Namastab: Transition into Decompose

by

Wesley Payton

The Downstate Illinois Series, Book 4

Namastab: Transition into Decompose

Cover Art by *The Wild Rose Press, Inc.*

The Wild Rose Press, Inc.
PO Box 708
Adams Basin, NY 14410-0708
Visit us at www.thewildrosepress.com

Publishing History
First Edition, 2023
Trade Paperback ISBN 978-1-5092-4488-1
Digital ISBN 978-1-5092-4489-8

The Downstate Illinois Series, Book 4
Published in the United States of America

Dedication

For Brian Federmeier, my friend and fellow scout.

Part One

Chapter 1

Weston and H.P. took their seats on the stage after giving a brief acceptance speech at the Prairie State Philological Society's annual Writers Roundup awards ceremony. H.P. examined the inscription on the small plaque they'd just received. "I wish I hadn't let you talk me into such a jokey title…it only vaguely relates to what the book is actually about."

"Why are you complaining?" asked Weston, sotto voce. "That title got the readers' attention—it's fun to say, and our book together outsold the last two we wrote separately combined…you know what I mean."

"I hear what you're saying, but now that the title is engraved on a plaque it makes our book seem…trivial."

"I'll tell you what's trivial." Weston took the plaque and pointed to his name listed under H.P.'s. "You got top billing. We both won the Co-Authored Illinois Book of the Year in the Romantic Suspense category; you'd think for such a prestigious award, they'd make the plaque a little bigger so they could put our names side by side."

"Well, I did write the lion's share of the book."

"You're doing your share of the lyin' all right. You may've done most of the typing, but without me there wouldn't have been many ideas for you to type up."

"If I'd only typed up your ideas, our entire book

would've been dialogue…just characters rambling on back and forth with the reader asking page after page, 'Is this going anywhere?' "

"Is that a fact?"

"No," H.P. answered, "it's a certainty."

"With that attitude, I have my doubts about whether you deserve to share this plaque with me."

"The last plaque I won, you were prepared to give away to a bartender who didn't want it, but now you intend to keep this one all to yourself?"

"You can have a turn, but I assume you'll want to hang it on the wall next to the last one in that dank and dinky office of yours across the quad rather than at your home where no one but you will ever see it, and since it's nearly winter break, I thought I'd take the first turn as your office is about to be closed for the better part of a month."

H.P. sat back in his folding chair. "That makes sense and yet simultaneously seems very self-serving."

"Shh," hissed the state's most successful adult coloring-book author, who sat directly behind them.

"Don't mind her," whispered Weston. "She's just pissed that they put her in the second row with all the print journalists."

The coloring-book author leaned forward, the wide brim of her straw hat scraping H.P. across the back of his neck. "Would you two kindly stop your nattering. The emcee is about to announce the state's new poet laureate."

Weston elbowed H.P. hard in the ribs. "Hey, look who it is waiting in the wings…that's the heiress."

The sight of the attractive, middle-aged woman made H.P. forget about his straw allergy and the sting of

Weston's oddly sharp elbows. "That's her? Introduce us at the reception afterwards."

"I thought we weren't going to that…besides, she's practically royalty now. Does one curtsy or bow to a poet laureate?"

"I'm sure she's still grateful to you for figuring out a way to save her father's favorite horse," said H.P. "I ask so little of you—can you just do me this one favor? I'll let you keep the plaque."

"Fine, but maybe don't mention that I came up with the idea to save her father's horse. I'm sure it must still be a sensitive subject for her."

****

H.P. rubbed the back of his neck as he and Weston stood in the informal queue to felicitate the new poet laureate of Illinois.

"Are you nervous or something?" asked Weston.

"No, my neck is itchy from the lady's hat that scraped against me."

"Pull yourself together…you look like you're scratching fleas."

Weston and H.P. took a step forward when the chancellor and her husband departed after conveying their compliments. "Hello again, Weston."

Weston shook the heiress's hand. "It's good to see you under better circumstances, Ms. Hedonia."

"Call me Anne, but please—no jokes about my name…I doubt I'd find any pleasure in the humor."

"Well, if humorlessness is what you're into, then you really ought to meet my writing partner, H.P."

Anne shook H.P.'s hand. "It's lovely to make your acquaintance."

"You're lovely too—nope, it's lovely to meet you

3

too…sorry about that."

Weston clapped H.P. on the shoulder. "You'll have to forgive my friend. He's received so many awards of late, that he often doesn't know whether he's coming or going at these things."

"Yes, my congratulations to you both. I was quite pleased when I heard your names announced; I very much enjoyed reading your book. I've read a few of Weston's before; however, H.P., this was the first time I'd read a book featuring your Pirate Hunter—such a marvelous character…so fearless and decisive, but I heard through the literary grapevine that you intend for this to be your last Pirate Hunter story."

"I'm afraid so…at least, I'm pretty sure."

Anne shook her head. "More's the pity."

"It's us who should be congratulating you," said Weston. "Today we were one of many award recipients, but you've received a most rarefied honor."

"I suspect the honor was bestowed upon me more for my philanthropy than my poetry. Frankly, the world no longer needs poetry, but somehow it still needs the occasional poet…someone the state can call on to be its poet laureate, or otherwise they'd have to revoke the position, and how would that look in the tourism brochures?"

H.P. nodded. "I completely agree."

"Me too," added Weston. "Unless it rhymes, I have a hard time even reading a poem."

H.P. rolled his eyes. "No, you philistine, I meant I agree that it's a shame more people don't respect the power of poetry."

"Yes, it is a shame." Anne smiled. "Though the nice thing about selling so few chapbooks of my poetry is that when somebody tells me they've read my book, and I say, 'So you're the one,' they can't accuse me of false modesty."

H.P. guffawed. "I think that's hilarious."

Weston shook his head. "We surmised as much from that girlish giggle of yours."

"I think you have a charming laugh," said Anne. "It puts me in a convivial frame of mind, as if I were attending a wedding reception. Apropos of matrimony, I understand that a former employee of my dad's is due to marry a friend of yours, Edwin Hubert."

"That's right," Weston replied. "Ed and Kate are planning to tie the knot on New Year's Day."

"How heartening—I recently became aware of the reason for Kate's resignation. I feel just awful about the whole affair. You two should bring your friend and his fiancée as well as your significant others up to my dad's…well, my house next weekend for a meditation retreat before all the craziness of the wedding. I've had the stables converted into a yoga studio."

Weston frowned. "Yoga and meditation are usually the types of activities that compel me to retreat."

"I also have a gifted gourmet chef on staff in addition to a well-stocked wine cellar."

"I suppose for Ed and Kate's sake, we could come up for a weekend visit."

"That sounds like a wonderful couples' getaway," H.P. said, "but regrettably I am unattached, so I'll respectfully decline so as not to be the cause for an uneven table setting."

Anne smiled again. "Nonsense. I'll be without a plus one myself, and I think you'd make a splendid dinner companion."

Chapter 2

Becky and Lance sat in the campus restaurant, waiting for their other dinner companions. She watched as her son squeezed the lemon from her iced tea into his glass of water and then poured in three packets of sugar. "You know, you could've just ordered a lemonade."

Lance stirred his drink with a butter knife. "Yeah, but this is fresh-made. The lemonade they serve here is probably from concentrate."

"I've seen you add mixed-berry Kool-Aid to milk to make blue milk; I don't think you get to be a connoisseur on unconcentrated beverages."

"I know what I like." Lance took the plastic ketchup bottle from the table and squirted in a long dash as he continued to stir, giving his drink a pinkish hue.

"You're quite the mixologist." Becky sipped her ungarnished iced tea. "So you've been in junior high for nearly a semester now. What's the biggest difference you've noticed between middle school and elementary school?"

"Deodorant." Lance drank down half his pink lemonade.

"Doesn't that taste a little…gross?"

"No, why should it? I like ketchup, and I like lemonade."

"Sure, but it's tomatoes and lemons—they don't exactly go together."

"They're both fruits. I don't hear you complain about that vegetable juice you drink every morning—which is a misnomer by the way since it's mostly tomato juice mixed with seven vegetables, so really it should be called fregetable juice or maybe vege-uit juice."

Becky smiled at her son. "I feel a complaint coming on now. Did you learn the word 'misnomer' at school?"

"No, from Weston."

"Well, next time he uses the word 'misnomer' you have my permission to kick him."

"That seems unkind."

"What's unkind is questioning the woman who gave birth to you." Becky looked up at the two men approaching. "Speak of the devil."

"Sorry we're late, Becca." Weston sat down and kissed Becky's cheek. "H.P. thought it prudent to make a brief appearance at the reception after the award ceremony."

H.P. stood behind the empty chair next to Lance. "Is this seat taken, Lancelot?"

"Rest your hippobottomus, hippopotamus."

H.P. sat down. "I assume you're referring to me as a hippo because of my initials."

"You got the 'ass' part right." Weston turned to the empty chair at the head of the table. "Where's Van?"

"Elsewhere it seems," answered Becky. "I've called his cellphone twice, but it goes straight to voicemail. I think we've been stood up."

Weston sighed. "That's rather rude. He's the one who picked this place."

"I was looking forward to seeing him," said Lance. "We haven't seen him since Thanksgiving."

H.P. unfolded his napkin to wipe up the droplets of

water and granules of sugar in front of him. "I saw him at the union last week…he seemed in good spirits."

The waiter approached with a couple of menus for the table's new arrivals. "Can I get you two something to drink?"

H.P. eyed Lance's glass. "I'll have the same as him."

Chapter 3

Lance slept in the backseat of the car as Weston drove back toward campus after having dropped H.P. off at his farmhouse. "Do you want me to stop by Van's dorm or head straight to your sister's to pick up Ance?"

"I don't know," Becky said from the passenger's seat. "Drive past his dorm...and we'll see if the light's on in his room."

"I'm not sure what that's going to tell us, but okay." Weston took a turn into a residential area filled with fraternity houses. "So are you excited about the couples retreat next weekend?"

"Sure, what's not to be excited about...private chef, expensive wine, massages."

"Anne didn't mention that she had a masseuse on her staff."

"I'm going with my husband—one way or another, somebody's going to rub my back."

"Just so long as you let me rub your front too."

Becky looked out the window at the large houses they drove past. "I can't remember the last time we made love in a bed that wasn't ours. Do you think Ed and Kate will want to go? It'd be kind of awkward if they didn't, though at this point I'd trade a weekend without kids for a little awkwardness."

"We'll know tomorrow when Ed gets back from Chicago with H.P.'s car, but I suspect they'll go. After all, Kate's between jobs and Ed's job is being an underemployed stargazer, so I think they can spare a couple of days." Weston slowed to a crawl as he drove along the street that ran behind Van's dorm tower. "Which one is his window?"

Becky leaned across her husband and looked up at the tall building. "Third floor from the top, fourth window from the right."

Weston counted down and then over. "His light is on."

"Should we drop in?"

"What if he's up there with a girl?"

"I'd prefer that to him not wanting to spend time with his mother."

"With all the practice he's had on his own, I suppose it's about time he had a partner, but still…he should have dinner with his family when they come to visit." Weston drove toward the parking lot. "Why don't you stay here with Lance, and I'll go talk to him?"

"Would you?"

****

Weston knocked on Van's door. "Entrevue," said the freshman from within.

Weston pushed open the door to find Van watching television from bed. "I hope you're not planning to major in French. 'Entrevue' doesn't translate as enter."

"What are you doing here?"

"The better question is: what are you doing here?"

Van sat up on his bed. "That's the same question."

"But I'm the one asking it…you were supposed to meet us for dinner."

"I totally forgot."

Weston took a seat on the desk chair. "Did you also

totally forget to check your phone over the past few hours, because you'd probably be the only teenager in America to do so. Your mom left you a couple of messages."

"Sorry."

"You don't have to apologize to me, but Lance was really looking forward to seeing you."

"I'll make it up to him when I come home for winter break."

"What's going on with you…why'd you bail on us tonight?"

Van turned his attention back to the television on the desk. Weston turned it off and folded his arms. "I never really felt good about myself—you know, over the long term—until I became a dad. I'd been in love before, but it was always a selfish sort of love with someone who made me feel better about myself, because they chose me. Your children don't choose you and sometimes they can make you feel bad, but you love them regardless…unselfishly, which ironically makes you feel good."

"Great story," said Van. "My favorite part is when it was over. Why are you telling me this anyway? You're not my dad."

"And yet I love you just the same."

Van looked out the window. "I'm failing. I came here as an Ag major so that I could transfer into the Engineering school, but I can't even hack it as a wannabe farmer."

"You've got finals coming up. Put the TV in the closet and buckle down. You owe it to yourself to at least try."

"Even if I aced my finals, which isn't going to

happen, I still couldn't raise my grades enough to switch majors, so not only will I have wasted this semester, but it'll take me two or three more semesters of really good grades just to make up for this one."

"You're not being smart," said Weston.

"Gee, thanks for the pep talk."

"I'm not saying you're not smart. I'm saying you're not being smart. You're so concerned about what may or may not happen in the future that you're not taking care of business right now in the present."

"All these other kids…they're so much better at this than I am."

"Because most of them came from schools in the suburbs where students are expected to go to college. They've been preparing to be here for the past four years. The priority of your small-town high school was to keep students from dropping out and to keep them from beating each other up."

"So you're saying I'm screwed."

"No, I'm saying high school is over—leave it behind. It's time to rise to the occasion. I know that you can. There's nothing your classmates are capable of that you aren't—it's just that they have more practice studying, but you deserve to be here the same as them. You raised your high school GPA and stuck with 4-H, so do it again…work hard and stick with it."

Van looked at Weston. "That's it, huh?"

"It might be difficult, but it's not complicated…though, of course, you could always move back home and get a job baling hay. It really just depends on what sort of hard work you're willing to do."

"I get what you're getting at."

Chapter 4

Anne sat behind the massive, double-pedestal desk her father had bought back in the '70s. She thought it too soon to redecorate her dad's office. The out-of-date furniture comforted the employees who came in to meet with her and, she suspected, helped to support her legitimacy to the throne, as it were. She didn't have the slightest idea how to edit DNA sequences, but she shared DNA with the man who founded the company. Still, if she had her druthers, she'd redo the entire office in a neo-art-deco style. "Where are we at with the Alzheimer's research?"

"My department has some promising leads," said the female vice president sitting in one of the three wingback chairs across the desk.

"My dad had been telling me about those promising leads for decades. When is the promise going to finally pay off?"

The vice president shifted in her chair. "Uh…probably not for another decade or so."

"Well, keep at it…that's why he started the company." Anne turned her attention to the other vice president. "How are things coming along with cleaning up your disgraced former colleague's mess?"

The balding man turned to the empty wingback where the company's third vice president had once sat for these quarterly update meetings. "It's a mess all right.

Just when I think I have all the cobwebs cleared out, I find a new strand that leads to a whole other web. Some of the offsite experiments he was running don't seem to have any discernable purpose—just dark science in the hopes that something might stick, and if any of it ever did, I have no idea what he planned to do with it."

"Maybe you can ask him when he gets out of prison in thirty to forty years." Anne closed the leather-bound notebook on her desk. "Okay, carry on. Obviously, we're not the only party looking for these shadow experiments of his, but the more we find and shut down first, the faster we'll salvage this company's flagging reputation—just remember to apprise our law enforcement contacts of any new findings."

The male vice president sighed. "I'll continue the housecleaning and keep following the strands."

"I know you won't let me down." Anne stood and then her two vice presidents, as well as the four assistant VPs seated behind them on a long couch, rose to their feet. "We'll meet again next week to finalize plans for the end-of-the-year board meeting."

"We'll be ready," said the female vice president.

"I have every confidence that you will be," replied Anne.

As the six suits left her office, Anne's executive assistant entered with a covered plate. "I took the liberty of ordering you sushi for lunch."

"I usually have soup when it's this cold."

"Yes, but you have that other meeting in a few minutes, and I didn't figure you'd want to slurp soup through it."

"It seems all I do these days is have meetings, and my primary function in them is to say, 'keep at it' and 'carry on.' " Anne uncovered the plate, which contained a light and dark maki roll curled into a circle to form a yin-yang symbol with a dollop of wasabi and a small mound of pickled ginger in the middle. "Yin and yang is a Chinese concept; sushi is Japanese."

"Shall I convey your critique to the kitchen?"

Anne shook her head. "No…at least they're being creative, instead of serving the same old tuna-fish sandwiches."

"The employees do seem to appreciate the cafeteria's new offerings."

"I suppose that's something I can be proud of."

"I think you can be proud of more than that." The executive assistant walked toward the door. "I'm sure the employees will also appreciate their Christmas bonuses that you authorized yesterday."

"It's been a good year…mostly." Anne followed her to the door. "Is everything ready for this weekend?"

"Yes, all the arrangements have been made and the forecast remains unchanged."

"Perfect." Anne locked the door behind her assistant and returned to her desk. She pulled her cellphone from her pocket, scrolled to the contact for Zeta Dry Cleaners, and then sunk into her chair. "Hello."

"Hello," replied the moderator. "With you present, we now have a quorum in our virtual meeting room, so we may begin. Per your instructions, our clearinghouse of clandestine chemistry continues to clean house."

"Excellent." Anne tore open a packet of soy sauce. "On my end, we're continuing to dismantle the armature of secret labs and ongoing experiments that were being run through this company."

"I still have concerns about this course of action,"

said a female voice. "We're effectively throwing away any progress we've made over the past few years."

Anne had grown weary of this now familiar tune. "That's correct…and exactly how much progress would you say has been made over the past few years?"

The female voice huffed. "This organization has made many advancements—"

"Sorry," interrupted Anne, "I appropriated your term 'progress' when I should've used one of my own. How much profit has this organization made over the past few years?" Anne paused to allow the ensuing silence maximum penetration. "The downside of having a non-scientist like me lead this organization is that I don't understand the objectives behind most of the experiments you've chosen to fund; the upside is that I don't care. This secret society was founded for two reasons: to take aggressive action behind the scenes in order to improve civilization through chemistry and to make money. So far as I can tell, heretofore it's accomplished neither. You scientists, with your pet projects that would never be sanctioned by any governing body or bear up to the scrutiny of even the most milquetoast of ethics probes, have simply lost your way. I'm probably the only person in this organization who has reviewed all the different projects that've been underway for the past few years, and I'm here to tell you that they don't make sense—not because I'm a layperson, but because they're pointless…you're just too deep down the rabbit hole to see it. No, we'll stay the course and continue to burn everything to the ground. Then as the authorities—whose attention you've attracted with your sloppy practices—sift through the ashes, we'll rebuild where no one will think to look for us."

"And that's what you're doing at your father's company now that you are in charge?" asked a male voice.

"Yes," Anne answered. "I've tasked a complete incompetent with the dismantling, ensuring that the authorities will have months if not years of new findings to keep them occupied."

"It's not that I doubt your commitment," said the female voice, "but you've still yet to fully articulate your plan for our rise from the ashes, so to speak, not to mention how you intend to keep our operation out of the searchlight, especially now that there are those who know enough to look for it."

"I intend to address that issue this very weekend."

Chapter 5

As he pulled onto the offramp from the interstate, Weston glanced in the rearview mirror at his car's crowded backseat, with Kate wedged in between Edwin and H.P. "Are you doing okay back there, Kate? We can stop and have one of the boys switch seats with Becca."

"No, I'm fine," said Kate. "This middle seat's just a bit bumpy is all, but it's not that far from my condo to my boss's old house. Besides, this definitely beats riding in the trunk…trust me, I know whereof I speak."

"Yes, thanks for picking us up," Edwin added.

Becky twisted around to face the occupants of the backseat. "You two are doing us the favor. After all, you're the reason we were invited, so it'd be a little uncomfortable to pull up without you."

"I'm glad it works out for all of us then," Kate replied. "As you might imagine, I wasn't looking forward to the prospect of driving past my previous place of employment in the very vehicle used in my abduction. Every time I put groceries in the trunk, I look over my shoulder to make sure nobody's going to push me in with my shopping bags."

"Why don't you just sell that car?" asked H.P.

"It's a lease," answered Kate, "and I've only got a couple more months left on it."

Weston looked in the rearview mirror again. "I'm sure they'd let you trade it in early for something else."

"I suppose," said Kate, "but I'm really not sure what sort of vehicle I'd be in the market for. All my focus right now is on marrying Eddie at the end of the month. This is the first time in my life that I don't have any idea what's going to happen next…and I kind of like the feeling."

"That sounds so exciting," replied Becky. "If you didn't want to return to the private sector, I'm sure the university would be glad to have you back."

Kate frowned. "Perhaps, but ever since the grievous incidents of earlier this year, I've sort of lost my faith in science…or at least the application of it. It seems even the work done by non-profit organizations often gets coopted and exploited at some point to make money for other entities with dubious motives."

"Since Ed's dabbled in your field," said Weston, "you could always take a crack at astronomy or cosmology or whatever the hell he does."

H.P. leaned forward to look over at Edwin. "Yeah, I'm a bit surprised you haven't tried to abscond with her to some isolated observatory and set up camp anew."

"The thought has crossed my mind, but neither of us have much family, so we're looking forward to celebrating our matrimonial merging with all of you; however, I'm thinking of a protracted equatorial honeymoon during which we'll visit several remote telescopes."

Kate smiled. "When Eddie promised me the stars and long, hot nights—I should've known better."

"That still sounds romantic to me," said Becky. "Though having an almost two-year-old lowers the romance bar a bit. These days, my idea of a romantic evening is a night without screaming."

Chapter 6

Weston and company pulled up in front of the sprawling ranch house as snow began to fall. "It looks like we arrived just in time."

"Yes, but will we be able to depart when it's time?" asked Kate.

Becky turned to reply. "I wouldn't mind being snowed in for a long weekend at a mansion with a gourmet kitchen and a wine cellar."

"It was also snowing last time we were here," Edwin observed.

Weston and H.P. exchanged a glance in the rearview mirror. "Oh, you mean last time the three of us drove up to Chicago together."

Edwin looked over at H.P. "Yes, I suppose that's what I mean."

Weston depressed a button on the console to pop the trunk lid. As the five climbed out of the sedan and began unloading things from the trunk, Anne emerged from the house, followed by two domestic servants. "I'm delighted that you made it before the snow started to fall in earnest. The groundskeeper will help with your bags, and the steward will show you to your rooms. I thought we'd have a light lunch in the solarium once you're settled."

"That sounds delicious," said H.P.

Anne grinned. "But I haven't told you what we're

having."

Weston handed H.P. his messenger bag. "He's not picky. He regularly eats dorm food on campus."

"I'm afraid it's true."

"Most of my meals come from the cafeteria at the office," Anne replied. "I just keep the chef on because he worked for my dad for so many years…but lately he mostly cooks for the staff."

H.P. walked with Anne toward the house. "That's very kind of you to keep your father's staff employed."

"I think it's what he would've wanted. He spent a lot of time here, and I can still feel his presence, so I abhor the idea of this old house sitting empty."

"I know just what you mean. I live in an old house out in the country myself."

Kate and Becky shared a smile as they followed H.P. and Anne up the walkway. The servants carried two bags each and walked behind them. Edwin lingered for a moment at the car as Weston closed his trunk. "Should I not have mentioned that we've been here before?"

"It's not like a state secret or anything," answered Weston, "but it's the kind of comment that invites a lot of questions—sort of an awkward conversation to be having as we pull up. 'Good to see you again, Anne. We were just talking about the last time we came here when we snuck onto the property and saw your father right before he died.' "

"Ah, I understand. I'm lucky to have a friend like you who's so adept at always knowing the right things to say."

"It's what I do best."

Chapter 7

Weston, Becky, Edwin, Kate, and H.P. entered the solarium and looked up at the heavy snow falling on the glass roof.

"It's like we're in a snow globe," said H.P.

Weston shook his head. "Then it'd be snowing inside—not outside. No, it's more like we're in a glass coffin being pooped on by a flock of diarrhetic pigeons flying overhead."

"And people say I'm a poet." Anne approached the group from behind with a tray of cucumber sandwiches. "Sorry to sneak up on you, but I let most of the staff leave early on account of the impending snowstorm, so lunch will be a buffet."

"This room is exquisite," said Becky, "though so is everything of this house that we've seen so far."

Anne set the tray on the sideboard. "Thank you. Dad liked to have lunch out here every day so he could feel the warmth of the sun."

"Is this the house you grew up in?" asked H.P.

"No, we had a place in the city, but when Dad's company started growing, he relocated his labs out here near the interstate and bought this property nearby to raise horses. We used to come out here on the weekends to ride, but then when Mom passed and I went off to college, he had this house built. It was sort of his retirement project, though he never exactly retired. I would tease him for building such a large house after I'd left home, but this place was really more of a hotel. He insisted that anyone who came to visit his company stay here rather than drive to find lodging."

"He was a very generous man," said Kate.

"Yes, even during the difficult times in his life, his concern was always for others."

Edwin eyed the sandwiches. "So…should we eat then?"

"Of course—please help yourself. The chef will be along in a moment with the salads, and then he'll finish prepping our dinner before he leaves for the day. I thought after our repast we'd go out to the yoga studio for a virtual session with a yogi who studied under Maharishi Mahesh. I stop in for a live session at his studio whenever I'm on the West Coast."

Weston smiled. "To paraphrase the only famous yogi I know, 'Yoga is ninety percent mental and the other half physical.' "

Anne smiled. "A Yogi Berra reference?"

"That's right," Weston answered. "Speaking of baseball, I happened to notice a rec room down the hall from our bedroom that contained some old baseball memorabilia. Your father's I take it."

"Yes, he played shortstop back in college, though thankfully for the field of neuroscience he wasn't quite good enough to turn pro."

"The room also had a pretty nice ping-pong table," said Weston. "Do you mind if me and the boys play a few games while you gals do your yoga thing?"

Becky frowned. "Our yoga thing? You know we have a ping-pong table at home in the garage."

"Yeah, but it's usually covered in junk...plus it's cold out there."

Chapter 8

Becky and Kate marveled at the expansive yoga studio as the overhead LED lights came to life. "When you mentioned this place used to be a horse barn, I was expecting something more…rustic."

Kate nodded. "I feel like we're inside a tastefully appointed starship."

"Thanks," said Anne. "I've kept the house just as it was when Dad lived there, but this space…well, I've made it my own. Room, raise the temperature 35 degrees."

"Are you talking to us?" asked Becky. "Is there a thermostat where I can turn up the heat?"

Anne chuckled. "No, sorry—I was talking to the room…you just have to say 'room' and then state your command."

Kate unzipped her sweatshirt. "I can feel it getting warmer already."

"I hope you're both okay with Bikram yoga…it always makes me feel like a hothouse flower—in the best possible way."

Becky took off her warm-up jacket. "I wouldn't mind feeling like an exotic flower for a little while."

"If either of you get thirsty, the beverage fridge in the corner is stocked with some sports drinks and several kinds of water. Room, video screen on." The twelve-foot landscape mural on the far wall suddenly dissolved into pixels to reveal another studio with a well-proportioned, shirtless man standing in its center. "Good afternoon, Panta."

Panta bowed. "Good almost afternoon here, Ms. Anne."

"I'd like to introduce you to a couple of my new friends, Kate and Becky."

"A pleasure to virtually meet you both." Soft sitar music started playing. "Let's begin with some breathing exercises. Please join me in Sphinx pose." Panta took position on the floor to demonstrate. He studied the three women as they followed his example. "Remember to stretch out your spine and take slow, controlled breaths."

As Becky and Kate bent themselves into the pose, they watched Anne in the mirror lithely arch her back as if her vertebrae had recently undergone a thorough lubrication.

Panta stared deep into the camera as if he were transporting himself to their location from half a continent away. "Very good…all of you. Kate and Becky, be sure to raise your shoulders with your entire body—not just your arms."

As Becky tensed her muscles, she felt the tenseness in the rest of her body dissipate—the positive tension replacing the negative.

"How do you feel?" asked Panta.

"A bit creaky," answered Kate.

"Then let's turn over and transition into crab pose."

"Okay," replied Kate, "but I'm a little afraid my shell might crack."

Panta adroitly contorted his body so that his torso rose above his shoulders and hips. "Push to the point of discomfort but no further."

Becky struggled with the pose, but her body slowly took the shape of an arc. "I feel about as flexible as a crustacean."

Kate admired her form from upside down. "You look like a tunnel, whereas I'm more of a bridge."

"At least you both can allow passage under," said Anne. "I imagine if the fellas were here, they'd still be flat on their backs."

Becky exhaled deeply. "Sometimes that's not such a bad position for a man to be in."

Chapter 9

Edwin perused the pennants and photos that hung on the wall, as Weston and H.P. paddled a ping-pong ball back and forth.

"What do you think the ladies are up to now?" asked H.P.

"Probably twisted into knots out in that dusty barn chanting namaste or maybe chatting about free-verse poetry," Weston answered.

"I'm glad you suggested this instead." Edwin leaned closer toward the wall to inspect a signature on a framed baseball card. "My plan had been to fake an injury to get out of doing yoga."

H.P. grabbed the ball as it bounced off the floor after missing the table. "What's your go-to malady these days?"

"My wrist," answered Edwin. "It elicits a lot of sympathy from Kate since I sprained it attempting to effect her rescue from that train earlier this year. It really does bother me sometimes on cold days like today."

"I hear you," said Weston. "I still get phantom pains from my missing toe when I walk on ice."

H.P. noticed Weston and Edwin staring at him expectantly. "My injuries are more emotional in nature."

Edwin shook his head. "The chill in the air has me feeling somewhat peckish."

"The finger sandwiches weren't to your liking?"

H.P. asked.

"They were tasty enough, but I was so hungry I could've eaten a whole arm. I think I'll wander down to the kitchen to see if the chef is still here. Perhaps I can convince him to make me a veggie Dagwood sandwich."

Weston readied himself for the next serve. "Yell if you get lost."

Edwin exited the rec room and took a left at the end of the long hallway. He followed his nose and eventually found the darkened kitchen. He flicked on the rows of overhead lights, revealing the dimensions of the kitchen, which was big enough to accommodate the staff of a mid-sized restaurant. The scent that had beckoned him came from a bank of ovens, the first of which contained a large roast. He walked over to a tall pot simmering on the nearby range. He lifted the lid to inspect its contents. The soup smelled delectable, but the broth was so thick that he couldn't tell if it was vegetarian. He turned his attention to two refrigerators along the opposite wall. The first contained mostly bottled beverages—the second raw ingredients, such as an enormous tub of butter and a few dozen eggs. A large, translucent container in the back caught his attention. *It looks like more soup...maybe borscht or gazpacho, but if it's borscht it could be made with a meat stock.*

Edwin didn't think anyone would mind if he took a bowlful for himself—there was so much, but then he thought better of it as he considered the mess he might make when pouring out the soup; he didn't know where to begin looking for a ladle or a bowl for that matter, so he shut the fridge door and searched for the pantry. He located the double-door pantry at the far end of the kitchen.

"Eureka!" Edwin was pleased to find several boxes of crackers and cookies. He took one of each, closed the pantry doors, and turned off the overhead lights. As he returned in the direction from which he came, it occurred to him that perhaps he ought to first stop by his room and drop off one of the snacks for later in case he found dinner to be likewise insufficient. *Yes, I'll share the crackers and keep the cookies for myself.*

Chapter 10

Weston and Becky entered the formal dining room to find H.P. and Anne standing near the picture window, admiring the warm colors of the setting sun reflecting off the snow-covered pastureland that stretched to the horizon.

Anne turned to greet her guests and took note of Becky's dress and Weston's tie. "Don't you two look smart?"

"It's not very often Weston hears that," said H.P.

"I see you're wearing your standard-issue tweed jacket," replied Weston. "You certainly get a lot of mileage out of that particular garment—no wonder you've had to patch the elbows."

Kate and Edwin entered from the other end of the room. Kate instantly noticed that everyone had dressed for dinner. "See, I told you that you should've put on a shirt."

"I'm wearing a shirt," Edwin protested.

"You're wearing a sweatshirt. I meant a shirt with buttons."

Anne gestured toward the long table with six place settings. "I've always believed that dinner jackets and dresses were meant to impress the help, and since I've sent them all home, your evening attire is entirely appropriate. Please have a seat everyone…I'll serve."

Edwin sat down first. "What are we having?"

"My four favorite foods," Anne answered. "All international fare. For the soup course, I'll be serving poisson velouté. For the main course, Wagyu rib-eye roast with poutine on the side. And for dessert, German chocolate cake, which actually was invented by an American baker with the surname German, but it's delicious so who cares where it comes from?"

"Does the soup in the fridge also happen to be poisoned?" asked Edwin. "I did a little foraging earlier in your kitchen."

Kate put a hand on her fiancé's shoulder. "Despite being a man of prodigious appetites, Eddie is a vegetarian."

"My apologies," said Anne. "I should've asked if any of you had dietary restrictions before you arrived. I'm afraid the fish soup is the only soup we have."

"Are you sure? I thought I saw a large container of—"

"No," interrupted Anne. "You must be mistaken. The chef clears the house's weekly menu with me…perhaps it was a leftover sauce of some sort."

"No matter," Edwin replied. "As long as I can have seconds or maybe thirds of the poutine sans gravy and cake, you'll hear no complaints from me."

Weston chuckled. "And that's how you make a chubby vegetarian."

Kate squeezed Edwin's cheeks. "My New Year's resolution is for Eddie to lower his BMI by twelve percent."

"Sounds like it'll be a short honeymoon," said Weston.

Chapter 11

The cake crumbs and spilled wine on the white linen tablecloth attested to the dinner party's enjoyment of their epicurean evening.

Becky set her notched dessert fork on the small plate in front of her. "I can't remember the last time I've eaten so much or so well."

"I agree," said Kate, "but I hardly feel guilty about the decadent dinner given the intensity of our session with Panta."

Weston sipped his wine. "Panta...sounds like a drummer in a glam metal band."

"We worked up quite a sweat as well playing ping-pong," added Edwin.

"At least you were appropriately attired for that," Kate said, "though I do hope you didn't restrain your wrist engaging in all that vigorous exercise."

H.P. turned to Anne. "How often do you work out? You look so shapely...I mean, you look like you're in shape."

"Exercise helps to stave off depression," Anne replied. "If you know someone who's really fit, chances are that they're either depressed or narcissistic...or in my case, a bit of both."

"What do you have to be depressed about?" asked Weston. "You're a rich and famous poet."

"You're correct about the former but hardly the

latter. My problem is that I never wanted to be rich, and the only reason people might know me as a poet these days is because of my charity work, which mostly entails giving away my dead dad's money to causes he would've rolled his eyes at…so as a penance I keep watch over the company he built that I never had any interest in myself; however, as it happens, that detachment is an asset when compared to those with questionable agendas and concerning motives who would kill to have my job—trust me, I have plenty to keep me awake at night. Exercise and wine help me sleep, though the side-effects are that one makes me impatient and the other too liberal of tongue."

Weston nodded. "I've never personally been afflicted by the burden of wealth, but H.P. you were once a millionaire, weren't you?"

H.P. shrugged. "I was, briefly, a millionaire one and a half times over…at least on paper—then I took an out-of-town job as a creative writing instructor after a bad breakup and subsequently took a deep loss on a lakeside condo that was overpriced when I bought it at the height of the market."

Anne set down her wineglass. "The world is comprised of impecunious people and people terrified of becoming so."

"My friends' work notwithstanding, I find the advantage of contemporary literature is that you don't have to read very much of it to understand almost all of it," said Edwin, struggling to participate in the discursive, vino-fueled conversation. "It's as if most authors today have access to the same unpublished and unending novel, each taking turns to excise passages to pass off as their own."

"What if the gatekeepers are actually stupid?" Anne asked rhetorically. "What if the curators don't know any better than the rest of us? Unfortunately, the postmodern response to those questions causes more problems than it solves. We need new gatekeepers, not no gatekeepers, but in our self-published…post it online with your cellphone culture, there's simply too much noise—too many voices for anyone to be heard, so now context has eclipsed content. These days what one says is less important than if one speaks for a particular tribe—tribalism over truth. The original purpose of art was to give cavemen something pretty to look at in the firelight after a long day of hunting wooly mammoths and running from saber-toothed tigers. Art was meant to bring us together. Now we all feel so damn isolated that we just want to know if someone else out there believes what we believe…and who cares if those beliefs are worth believing in, since we're all being pursued by the same apex predator—only now, instead of saber teeth, it has cyber claws. The medium used to be the message. Now the medium is the means of mass extinction…or mass extinguishment perhaps, not of the flesh but of the soul."

Becky swirled her wine. "I have this co-worker who I detest. Whenever she offers an opinion, which is rare, she follows it with this silly little giggle, giving anyone within earshot permission to dismiss her opinion out of hand if they so wish. I don't think you two are related."

"This is all quite thrilling," said Kate. "It's been ages since I've heard anyone use the terms 'truth' or 'soul.' As a scientist, you tend to get laughed out of the room when discussing anything that can't be quantified and disaggregated."

"Yes, I'm enjoying our chat too," Anne replied. "However, it looks like we're out of wine, and I know I could use some coffee. So I'll pop into the kitchen to start a pot and then retrieve a couple more bottles of pinot noir from the cellar while it's brewing."

H.P. stood up. "Let me help you…to carry a pot of coffee and two bottles of wine, you'll need at least one extra hand."

Weston finished off the last of his wine. "And as luck would have it, you come with an idle pair."

Chapter 12

Edwin ran his finger around the rim of his wineglass, creating a high-pitched tone that he alone found pleasing.

"I believe you're demonstrating the reason stemless glassware was invented," said Weston.

Kate nodded. "Eddie dear, I agree with Weston's sentiment; I find that noise you're making quite noisome."

Edwin raised the glass to his lips. "Then I'll be glad to instead utilize this wine for its intended purpose, though if they don't soon return with another bottle, I'll begin to miss the jugs of this stuff that I used to buy."

Becky also drank down the last sip of her wine. "I wish we'd suggested that they make the coffee—or whatever—and the rest of us raid the wine cellar."

"We could go check on them and ask for the tour," said Kate.

"If I know H.P., he waited until they were in the cellar to make his move," replied Weston, "so I don't want to go interrupting his woo pitching, especially since he's had so little opportunity to pitch it of late."

Kate shook her head. "If it were me, I wouldn't find dusty bottles and cobwebs to be all that romantic."

"Of course not," Weston replied, "you're a reasonable woman, but trust me—H.P. has it in his head that women want nothing more than to be swept off their feet in crypt-like environs. You should hear what sort of activity he suggested that my Spinster and his Pirate Hunter get up to in such a setting."

****

Anne, standing in the cellar with her back against a large cask of wine, held up a bottle whose label H.P. ostensibly leaned in to inspect. "You know, in this light your eyes remind me of Marlene Dietrich's—bright with allure and yet dark with mystery."

"I'm curious, have you had a lot of success with that come on…comparing women to actresses from the silent film era?"

"Now that you mention it, none whatsoever." H.P. kissed Anne tenderly on the lips and then passionately on the neck.

"Whoa there."

"You didn't enjoy that?"

"Yes, I rather did, but I don't want to keep the others waiting."

"They've probably forgotten all about us," said H.P.

"I'm positive that they haven't."

"Either way, I'm sure they'd understand."

"Likely so, however they're your friends, but my guests." Anne placed a hand on H.P.'s chest. "Perhaps we could continue this later…though not in the wine cellar. It's creepy down here."

Chapter 13

Anne entered the dining room carrying a tray with a coffee service. H.P. followed behind with two bottles of red wine.

Weston eyed the bottles. "Seems like it took almost as long to brew that coffee as it must've taken to brew the wine."

H.P. set one bottle on the table and began uncorking the other. "Wine isn't brewed; it's vinified."

"My point still stands," said Weston.

"Since it's already standing, I encourage it to go take a hike," replied H.P. "Now who could use a refill?" Four wineglasses shot up.

Anne began pouring coffee. "Help yourselves to some java. There's cream here too, but I couldn't find the sugar. The staff sets up a coffee station each morning, and I'm not sure where they keep everything. Sometimes I still feel like a guest in this house."

"I'm surprised you didn't find some sugar downstairs." Weston winked at H.P. "Since, as I understand it, dry goods are often kept in cellars."

H.P. shook his head. "Then one would imagine it's not a suitable place to keep your liver."

"I don't drink too much." Weston lifted his refilled wineglass to his lips. "I just drink too often."

Anne sat down. "The byplay between you two is delightful…I could listen to it all night."

Becky chuckled. "You might feel that way for one night but trust me—day after day the jokes wear a bit thin."

"Isn't that so often the way," Anne replied. "What amuses in springtime grows tiresome by autumn...and Weston, since you seem inordinately curious—H.P. and I kissed in the cellar. It was quite nice."

Weston turned to the others. "See...I told you he has a thing for basements."

"A moment ago you mentioned feeling like a guest in this house," said Kate. "I'm sure it must be convenient living just down the road from your office, but do you still keep a place in the city?"

Anne stirred her coffee. "Jean Paul-Sartre believed that 'hell is other people.' The older I get, the more I'm inclined to agree with that perspective. I'm afraid I've outgrown city living."

Weston set his glass on the table. "Having left the city to move downstate just a couple of years ago, I can relate. In fact, I think most of us can."

Kate nodded. "Yes, I find myself in want of a bit more personal space of late too."

"Who could blame you?" asked Anne. "I'm so sorry my dad's company...my company was at all involved in what happened to you this past winter. I want you to know that since then we've hired a new security director who has updated our facility's safety and monitoring protocols, and of course I hope it goes without saying—though I'll say it anyway because I want it to be perfectly understood—you are most welcome to have your old job back anytime you want it. I don't have the first clue about the work you did for us, but by all accounts you were the best at it."

Kate smiled. "Thanks, that's very kind of you to say."

"I find it disturbing that a pair of bad guys were able to so easily infiltrate our supposedly secure labs." Anne sipped her coffee. "Weston...H.P., reading your last book made me wonder—why in adventure stories do the good guys regularly call the villains bad guys, but the bad guys never refer to the protagonists as good guys?"

Chapter 14

Weston held Becky in his arms under the bedcovers as they gazed out the window at the snow falling in the moonlight.

"What do you like most about me?" asked Becky.

"Your willingness to do what we just did."

"Stop...I'm being serious. I feel like an old married couple around the engaged Ed and Kate and the flirty Anne and H.P. It's been so long since I've heard you say tender things to me, and I get it...it's hard to say tender things while chasing after a toddler or helping a middle schooler with his homework, but for the first time in a long time it's just us—alone in an unfamiliar bedroom. So what do you see in me that's special?"

"I don't know," answered Weston.

"That's not very romantic."

"It is actually. I see how wonderful you are, of course—you're beautiful and clever and fun and kind. But everyone who knows you sees those things too. However, I see something special in you beyond that. Your je ne sais quoi, which translates as a quality that can't be easily described—and it's all around you, radiating from you like the light from that moon out there...an otherworldly magic that I have no trouble believing in even though I don't know exactly what it is. That's what I see when I look at my Becca."

She kissed the arm he'd draped over hers. "Okay,

that's pretty good."

"I think you're just saying that because you're a little tipsy."

"Maybe, but it's still nice to hear. I think everybody was a bit tipsy tonight...especially Anne, though it seemed like she had the least to drink of us all."

"I noticed that too," he replied. "She refilled her glass the fewest times, but by the end of the evening I think she'd scored the most non sequiturs."

"I'm glad she was able to blow off some steam. It seems like she has to deal with a lot of stress."

"Do you think H.P. paid a visit to her bedroom to help her undress and destress?"

"No...maybe." Becky pulled the sheet up to her neck. "I guess we'll know in the morning."

"Eggs over uneasy with a side of awkward bacon and a glass of aren't-you-going-to-say-anything juice."

"Speaking of something to drink, would you get me some water so that I don't wake up with a headache?"

"You expect me to go all the way down to the kitchen to fetch you a glass of water?"

Becky handed him her empty water bottle from the nightstand. "No, just fill this up in the bathroom sink for me."

Weston reluctantly took the bottle. "Merci beau-poop."

"There you go again trying to impress me with your French."

"I happen to be fluid in several other languages too." Weston got out of bed and attempted to turn on the light in the bathroom. "The bulb in here must be dead."

Becky looked again at the nightstand. "The alarm clock is off. I think the power is out. Can you hand me my cellphone from the dresser?"

"You're going to call someone to come fix the electricity? I doubt you'll get a signal all the way out here in this storm."

"No genius, I'm going to use my phone as a flashlight."

As Weston groped his way toward the chest of drawers, a shrill scream shattered the still of night.

Part Two

Chapter 15

H.P. sipped cold coffee from a paper cup. An overhead fluorescent bulb buzzed and flickered endlessly. The mostly silent interrogator who sat in the corner of the small room seemed irritated, while the other one across the table from H.P. appeared eager to fill his legal pad with notes. "I just want to make sure I have my timeline correct. The dinner party broke up a little after midnight, right?"

"That's one long-ass dinner." The reticent police officer leaned back in her chair.

"By that point, it was more of a drinking coffee and wine party taking place in a dining room," H.P. said, "but yes, we dispersed just after midnight."

The garrulous officer circled something on his yellow pad. "And remind me how you knew it was after midnight?"

"As I've told you twice before, the grandfather clock in the hallway tolled the hour, and a few of us remarked on the lateness of the evening."

"Time just got away from you, huh?" asked the sitting officer.

H.P. turned to look at her. "Yes, I guess it did...we'd been having a pleasant conversation—sort of the opposite of what you and I are having now."

The other officer flipped back a few pages. "Okay, so everyone departs for their bedrooms at…we'll call it 12:15. But then you come back out of your room about 1:00 a.m."

H.P. returned his attention to the interrogator across from him. "Yes, I'd been watching television when the power went out, so I went to check on Anne…Ms. Hedonia."

"I take it you and Ms. Hedonia were on a first name basis." The interrogator made a note in his pad.

"Yes, it was a lavish dinner party without being formal."

"I wonder," said the female detective, "why check on her instead of your friends who you came with?"

"Because they're all coupled, but I knew Anne was alone, so I thought it made sense to check on her first."

The male detective scribbled another note. "I suppose being alone in the dark would make her vulnerable."

"I wasn't concerned about her vulnerability so much as I didn't want her to be frightened. She'd mentioned earlier in the evening how she sometimes felt uneasy about being alone in such a large house."

The female detective nodded. "Maybe she also felt uneasy about unattached, overnight guests who'd had too much to drink wandering the halls."

H.P. turned toward her again. "I don't like what you're implying. I get that you're just doing your job, which as far as I can tell primarily involves slouching and being an asshole, but since we've already been over all this before, I submit that it's time for you to stop asking questions and start looking for Anne."

Chapter 16

Becky took as many notes as the male detective did, having borrowed a pen and legal pad for that purpose.

"Ms. Hernandez, let's continue from the power outage," said the male interrogator.

"It's Mrs. Payley," Becky corrected. "I've told you that three times already."

"Of course, my mistake." He flipped back a couple of pages in his notepad. "You mentioned that the power went out at approximately 1:00 a.m."

Becky shook her head. "I don't believe I did."

"So then you're disputing that the electricity went out at one?" asked the female detective.

"No, I'm saying that I didn't notice there was no electricity until about 1:30. As far as I know, it could've gone off any time after 12:30 or so."

"If there was no power, how do you know it was 1:30 when you finally noticed the outage?" asked the male detective. "You couldn't have seen a watch in the dark, and you stated the alarm clock in your room is electric."

"I saw the time on my cellphone," answered Becky.

"But you told us that you couldn't get a signal out there," said the female detective.

"That's correct, though the time function still works even if there isn't any cell service. No offense, but you don't seem very smart. From one professional woman to another, you do a disservice to us all when you take a position of public trust for which you're woefully unqualified."

"Let's return to the matter at hand and save the women's lib discussion for later," said the male interrogator. "So you heard the scream about 1:30?"

Becky nodded. "My husband got up to get me some water, the bathroom light was out, we heard the scream, he handed me my phone from the dresser, I saw that it was just after 1:30."

"How long after 1:30?" asked the female interrogator.

Becky flipped back several pages in her legal pad. "When you asked me that a half hour ago, I answered 1:34, which I'm sticking with."

The male officer made a note. "So the time of the scream was 1:34 then?"

"No, it was a couple of minutes before," answered Becky. "It took my husband some time to find my phone and then make his way back to bed in the dark."

"You mentioned before that you'd been drinking," said the male detective.

"Yes, that's correct."

"Were you or your husband drunk?" asked the female detective.

"No, if we were drunk, we would've been asleep by then."

The female detective shook her head. "I find it curious that you were awake from the time you returned to your room until the time you allegedly heard a scream about an hour later, but that you didn't hear any other noises before then or happen to notice that the electricity had gone out."

"And I find it curious that you were ever able to pass the detective's exam."

Chapter 17

Edwin drank down the last of his coffee and set the paper cup on the interrogation room table. "Is there any chance I could get a refill?"

"I can't remember anyone ever asking for a second cup," said the male detective. "Sure, we can get you some more coffee, but we're making solid headway here, so let's push on a little further before we take a break."

"Okay…maybe we could have a snack too during that break."

The female detective nodded. "I think that can be arranged."

"Splendid," Edwin replied. "You always hear about the good cop/bad cop dynamic in situations such as this, but so far you two have been quite genial."

The male interrogator consulted his notes. "Thank you, Mr. Hubert—that means a lot. So to recap, you awoke to the sound of screaming about 1:30 in the morning."

"No, Kate—my fiancée—woke me up, and I believe she just heard a single scream…not screaming."

The detective turned a page in his notepad. "Right, so you two go out into the hallway and meet up with Mr. and Mrs. Payley."

"That's correct, we spotted them down the hall because Becky was using her mobile phone like a flashlight."

"Then the four of you went to check on your friend H.P."

"But he wasn't in his room," added the female interrogator.

"Yes, though he soon returned…likewise using his mobile phone as a flashlight."

"Alone?" asked the male interrogator.

"Yes, he told us he'd gone to check on Anne when the power went out. Not finding her in her room, he went to search for her—apparently, they'd kissed earlier in the evening, so it wouldn't surprise me if he wanted to reconnect with her so that they might continue their amorous dealings."

"How did he seem to you?" asked the female detective.

"It was dark, of course, so I don't really know…though I have a difficult time reading people in broad daylight."

The male officer lowered his legal pad. "He didn't appear agitated in any way?"

Edwin shook his head. "No, not that I noticed."

"So then you all split up to continue the search for the source of the scream," said the female officer.

"That's right—Weston, Becky, and H.P. went to search the living room and the solarium, while Kate and I searched the dining room and the kitchen."

"But you didn't find anything." The male officer made a note in his legal pad.

"No, it's a big house…we kept calling out for Anne, though we never heard anything but each other, nor did we see anything that looked out of place as if there'd been a struggle."

"You think there might've been a struggle?" asked

the female officer.

"It seems likely. As I mentioned, I was sound asleep, so I didn't hear the scream, but my understanding is that people don't usually scream when they trip over an ottoman in the dark and knock themselves unconscious on the corner of a coffee table or something like that. Besides, I imagine you or other officers also searched the house this morning with the lights on, and since you're questioning me, I assume that you didn't find Anne either."

The male detective underlined something on his notepad. "That's a very logical assumption, Mr. Hubert."

Chapter 18

Kate studied the room as the female interrogator studied her and the male interrogator studied his notes. "Mr. Hubert told us that you woke him up after you heard the scream about 1:30 in the morning, is that correct?"

"For the third time now, I won't answer any questions without my attorney present," said Kate. "If you have some information to share with me, then I'm all ears, but otherwise we're done here."

"Why are you so anxious to lawyer up?" asked the female detective.

"Do you not understand what a question is?" asked Kate. "If you need a hint, what I just said was a question."

"How come you don't want to talk with us?" asked the male detective.

"See, that's another question. You two are really lousy listeners…so gosh, that might be one reason."

The detective set his legal pad on the table. "Why are you playing games with us? And I know…that was also a question."

"You think you're smarter than us?" asked the female detective.

"In all likelihood, but that's not at issue. I hope you don't take this personally, but I suspect you two are overworked and underpaid, and people only tend to value their work about as much as they feel valued.

However, on the other hand, being a detective comes with a certain cachet—both in the media, with its myriad depictions of intrepid investigators facing down perils to solve crimes, and in your work culture…I imagine that many of your subordinates on the police force aspire to one day have your jobs. So you see, it's a perfect storm of professional attenuation and social overinflation. Hubris is always dangerous, but hubris predicated on unrealistic expectations is more dangerous still. To maintain your status, you must close cases, but you're not given the time or resources to close them properly. So you'll twist whatever answers I give to your questions into the most plausible, jury of my peers—which they won't be—digestible narrative possible, and when the court returns a conviction your colleagues will pat you on the back and say 'well done.' "

"So why do you think you're smarter than us?" the male detective asked.

"I have no doubt that's another common strategy in you line of work…simply ignore answers that challenge your way of thinking and then redirect. I predict you'd have a bright future in politics, if you were so inclined."

The female detective rose to her feet and stood over Kate. "I hear everything you're saying, but I still don't believe that you're smarter than me."

"You might've heard me, but you clearly weren't listening. I've already told you that it doesn't matter if I am or if I'm not. However, since it obviously matters to you, let me ask you a question and don't take your eyes off me until you've answered. I've only ever been in this room once, whereas you've been in here many times before. How many electrical sockets are in here?"

The detective couldn't help but glance around the

room. "I…"

"The answer is two—one behind me and another behind your partner." Kate looked down at the notepad. "Why are legal pads yellow?"

The female detective sighed. "Okay, so you're smarter than me."

"Don't feel bad…I'm not going to brag about it to anyone—but believe me when I tell you that I'm smart enough not to answer your questions without my attorney."

"Why are legal pads yellow?" asked the male detective.

"No one knows for sure…either because yellow is easier on the eyes under bright lights or because it doesn't show its age as much as white paper."

Chapter 19

Weston stared at the female detective staring at him. "I'm so focused on not blinking that I can't remember which of us blinked last."

"I advise you take this a little more seriously," said the male detective.

"Take what more seriously? You asking me the same damn questions over and over without answering any of mine in return? Did you find Anne? If not, do you have any leads concerning her whereabouts?" Weston pointed at the mirror on the wall across from him. "And why do you call those two-way mirrors when only one side is a mirror and the other a window?"

"I'll answer your question if you answer mine first." The male detective consulted his notes. "I'd like some more clarity around the events just after the scream when your group congregated in the hallway."

"There's not much to tell," said Weston. "We all went out into the hall because we heard the scream…Becca and I went out first, then Ed and Kate exited their bedroom a moment later—and then H.P. joined us. It seems he'd already been looking for Anne."

"Before the scream?" asked the female detective.

"She speaks!" Weston turned his attention back to the female detective. "With that silent treatment, you really put the terror in interrogator. Yes, he was already looking for her…it seems they'd had a moment of ô là là earlier in the evening, so I suspect he was hoping to pick up where they'd left off."

"So you think they'd planned a rendezvous for later?" the male detective asked.

"I doubt they'd prearranged a tryst…probably more like he thought he'd knock on her door when the lights went out to see if she wanted any company."

The officer turned back a few pages in his notepad. "But he didn't find Ms. Hedonia in her room—or at all…at least that's what he told you when you discovered him roaming the halls moments after hearing the scream."

"Firstly, we didn't 'discover' him. Secondly, I wouldn't characterize him as 'roaming the halls'…he was as concerned as the rest of us—probably more so. Thirdly, I understand that you have to consider every possible angle in your investigation, but besides being a general pain in the ass, H.P. is about the nicest guy I know."

"So what happened next?" asked the female officer.

"Like I told you, we split up to find Anne. H.P. came with me and Becca, while Ed and Kate went the other direction. It's a big house, and it was dark of course, so we kept calling out for her, going from room to room, taking turns using our cellphones as flashlights."

"You didn't happen to find any actual flashlights or candles?" asked the male detective.

"Like a candelabra?" Weston shook his head. "No, it's a fancy house, though not…you know, Liberace fancy. We did find a flashlight in the laundry room, but the batteries were dead."

The female interrogator shifted in her chair. "So you left it there?"

"No, it was one of those heavy-duty deals…metal, so I kept it as a thumper just in case."

The male interrogator made a note. "Just in case of what?"

"I don't know…in case we came across somebody in the house who wasn't supposed to be there."

"But you never did?" the male officer asked.

"Oh, my apologies…last time I answered that same question did I leave out the part when we found a prowler, and I clonked him over the head with a flashlight?"

"There's no need for sarcasm, Mr. Payley." The officer made another note. "We just want to be sure we have a clear understanding of last night's events."

"Did anyone else have a 'thumper'?" asked the female officer.

"Yeah…H.P. had grabbed a baseball bat off the wall in the rec room when we searched there. When we met up later with Ed and Kate in the kitchen, Ed had a chef's knife."

"So the men were armed, but not the women?" asked the male interrogator.

Weston nodded. "Yes…I believe that's correct. Becca held the cellphone. She switched back and forth between hers and mine and then H.P.'s when our phones lost power, but by then we'd searched the whole house as best we could, and we wanted to be sure at least one of our phones still had enough charge in case we got a signal once the storm abated."

"And what about the others?" the female interrogator asked.

"Ed doesn't have a cellphone, so they would've used Kate's. They were already in the kitchen when we'd given up our search."

"Sounds like a pretty scary situation," said the male detective. "You never gave thought to leaving the house?"

"In a blizzard?"

"Maybe driving away," said the female detective, "or at least hiding out in your car?"

"It was covered under two feet of snow...there wasn't anywhere to drive, and if there had been someone else around, we would've made for easy targets in my snowbound car."

The male detective turned a page in his legal pad. "So you guys met up in the kitchen and ate cookies and crackers until the groundskeeper showed up in the morning with his snowplow-equipped truck?"

"Yep, that's about it. There wasn't much else to do, and stress eating seemed like a good way to calm the nerves as well as pass the time. We'd talked about going back to the cellar for a couple of bottles of wine, but even with the lights from our cellphones, it was awful dark down there, so none of us had the stomach for it. You know, that's probably the one place in the whole house we could've searched better. Did you guys have a thorough look in there?"

"So what's your theory then?" The male officer set his pen atop his notepad. "Where do you think Ms. Hedonia vanished to?"

"You two are the detectives, but if I had to hazard a guess, I'd say she was outside her bedroom—maybe looking for H.P.—when the lights went out. She got spooked by something in the dark and screamed, then hightailed it into a hidden panic room that we never happened upon. The only part that doesn't make sense is why she didn't reemerge, but maybe with the power out, she got locked in somehow. I don't know if you still have officers out at her house, but it wouldn't surprise me if they find her wandering through the living room later today." Weston sat up straight. "Okay, I've answered all your questions...again. How about you answer some of mine?"

"That seems fair enough." The male detective turned to the two-way mirror. "They're also called one-way mirrors, which to your point is a more accurate term since only one side is reflective. As to why they're sometimes called two-way mirrors...English is such an ad hoc language, rife with idiosyncrasies. Did you know, that even though they're spelled and pronounced the same, the word *mogul* meaning magnate has a Persian origin, while the word *mogul* meaning ski bump is German in origin." The detective pointed his index finger at the mirror and touched his fingertip to the glass. "Check this out—here's how you can tell if you're looking into a two-way mirror. If there's a space between your fingernail and its reflection, then it's a real mirror, but if the nails touch like on this one...then there could be someone watching from the other side."

Weston smiled and turned to the female detective. "He's a bit of a showoff, isn't he?"

Chapter 20

Weston, Becky, Edwin, Kate, and H.P. sat near the window of a diner at a long table with a lean man in a suit. Kate handed him a menu. "Can we buy you a late lunch for springing us from jail?"

The lean man shook his head. "No thanks, I'm having dinner with my in-laws in a couple of hours. Besides, none of you were under arrest…merely persons of interest being held for questioning, so all it took to 'spring' you was flashing my ABA credentials."

"What sort of attorney are you?" asked H.P.

"He's helped me protect a few of my chemical creations over the years," said Kate.

"You handle copyrights then." Weston furrowed his brow. "So you wouldn't be much use if they ever decide to charge any of us."

"I'm a patent attorney…you can't copyright a chemical formula, but no—I wouldn't be any good to you as a criminal defense lawyer." The lean man stood from the table. "Kate, I wish you the best. Let me know how this all shakes out…or if you need a referral."

Kate waved goodbye. "Yeah, I'll be in touch—thanks again."

Slim passed by the lean man as he approached the table. "Here y'all are."

"I'm glad to see you, young man," said Edwin.

"Where've you been?" asked Weston. "We could've

used your assistance like five hours ago."

Slim took the lawyer's seat. "If you're going to make a habit of getting into trouble with the law in upstate Illinois, you'll need to factor in my driving time."

"How'd you find us?" Becky asked.

"A friend of mine is a cop in these here parts. He remembered Weston's name from a couple of stories I might've mentioned, so he called this morning to tell me that you all was being held across the street at the station, but when I arrived I was informed that they'd cut you lose a little while ago...given that they impounded Weston's car as evidence and the lack of dining options in this here burg—well, narrowing my search didn't take much in the way of deduction."

"Then it sounds like you were the right investigator for the task," said Weston.

"Did they tell you anything?" asked Kate. "They didn't tell us a thing."

"At first, as a professional courtesy, a couple of cops at the front desk shared a few facts, but then everybody got real tight-lipped when them two detectives who interrogated you all asked who I was and where I was from."

"Do they have any idea how Anne's doing or where she is?" asked H.P.

"Yes and no," answered Slim. "They don't know where she is, but they know she's dead."

Becky turned to H.P. "I'm so sorry."

H.P. lowered his head. "How...how do they know she's dead if they can't find her."

"You all didn't leave the main house until the cops showed up, didja?" asked Slim. "Out in that barn, which from what I was told has been converted into some kind of exercise room, they found about a gallon of blood pooled on the floor. They had several samples of the blood analyzed on the double, given the high-profile nature of the disappearance, and it came back an hour ago as a perfect match for Ms. Hedonia's."

H.P. pulled a napkin from the dispenser. "But if there isn't a body...then maybe—"

"No," Kate interrupted, "the human body only holds four to six quarts of blood."

Slim nodded. "That's right—you lose more than a half-gallon of the stuff then you're definitely a goner."

"So do the cops have any theories?" asked Becky.

"Plenty," answered Slim, "and every one of them involves you all."

"But how," H.P. stammered. "I mean why would we—"

"You don't have to protest your innocence to me," Slim interrupted. "I know you all didn't do it, but if you look at it from their perspective...well, it paints a mighty peculiar picture. There was nobody else at the house but you all. The closest neighbor is the groundskeeper, who lives about a mile up the road, and there are no tracks—foot or tire—up to the house."

"But it began snowing as soon as we got there," said Becky.

Slim sighed. "True, which could explain how tracks might've been covered up later, but then on the other hand the houseworkers left just as the snow started really coming down, meaning the roads would've been impassable most of last night."

Edwin rubbed his chin. "So maybe someone drove up before then, hid until the power went out, did the deed and absconded with Anne's body...or left it somewhere out in the snow for that matter, then waited for the snowplows to clear the roads so that he could make good his escape."

"That makes sense, except for the alarm log records—right up until the moment when the power went out, you all were locked in." Slim placed his elbows on the table. "Also, the main breaker in the fuse box had been switched off, so the power didn't go out because of the storm."

"Then maybe someone slipped into the house before it got locked up for the night," Becky said, "and then hid until we were all asleep."

"Yeah maybe," said Slim, "but from what I was told, the security at that house is awful good. The only way in or out was through the front door—plus there's cameras everywhere."

"Is the fuse box in the cellar?" asked Weston.

"Yep," Slim answered. "I guess it's tucked behind some stairs…kinda hard to get to—the groundskeeper had to show the cops where it was."

Weston nodded. "That makes sense because we couldn't find it either. Like I told the detectives, that's the one place in the house we didn't search thoroughly on account of there were no windows to let in the moonlight, so it was dark as hell. I had thought maybe Anne concealed herself in a saferoom or secret passage as a precaution. Did the cops find anything like that?"

Slim shook his head. "No, as you might imagine, the disappearance of an heiress to a multi-billion dollar company with a bunch of government contracts is a big damn deal, so it's been all hands on deck out at the house since you all was brought in, and this ain't just some local matter. They got people out there with sonar equipment pinging the walls for that very sorta thing, but so far nothing—the house looks to be just as it appears in the original blueprints...no off-the-books add-ons."

Edwin took a sip of water. "With all those law enforcement agents working the case, I imagine they'll turn up some promising leads soon. Now that we've given our statements to the authorities, do you think they'll need to question us further?"

Slim tilted his head back. "Ed, I don't think you quite get what's going on here. You are their prime suspect, and that ain't an easy designation to shake."

"Why are we the prime suspects?" asked Edwin. "There's no evidence that we did anything wrong."

"That's not entirely accurate," Slim replied. "And when I say 'you' I mean specifically you, Ed. I told you about them cameras...it seems they got one outside the entrance to that converted barn, and they have video of you lurking around in the woods nearby."

Edwin set his waterglass down. "But I—"

"No, I know," interrupted Slim. "My best guess is that it's footage from earlier this year that's been edited in...when it was also snowing, if you recall."

"So I'll just explain to them—"

"Explain what, Ed?" asked Weston. "That you were where you had no business being the same day Anne's father was found dead? Even if the cops believe you, I doubt it'll help your cause."

"But yesterday I was with others the whole time inside the house," said Edwin.

"Oh crap." H.P. put his hand to his forehead. "That's not exactly true—remember, you went to get a snack while we were playing ping pong...which I mentioned to the detectives."

Weston shook his head. "Nice job, Judas."

"I didn't know at the time that they considered any of us suspects," replied H.P. "I was just answering their questions so that they might somehow use the information to find Anne."

Edwin leaned back. "But I just went to the kitchen...I didn't leave the house. They don't have me on camera exiting the front door."

"Not likely," Slim said, "but they might just interpret that to mean that you'd discovered a way to get in and out undetected. This is one of those times when being smart counts against you. Listen, my sense is that they ain't got all the finer points worked out yet, and they won't charge you until they do, but my gut tells me that they're building a case against you five with Ed as the ringleader. They probably figure you all, whodunnit writers and whatnot, were engaging in some sort of modern-day Leopold and Loeb scenario—committing a murder just to see if you could get away with it...maybe they even think that you're somehow behind everything that's happened over the past couple of years. You've got to admit it's mighty strange how y'all keep getting targeted by this shadow outfit that nobody else seems to know much about."

"Even if any of that were true," Edwin replied, "without a body all the police have is circumstantial evidence that we were involved in a murder, so I like our chances."

"I don't." Slim sat back. "No offense, but your artism condition or whatever it's called probably didn't help you none. I suspect that those detectives read your tone—this tone here of sounding unconcerned—as taunting them to play your game."

Edwin hung his head. "I've learned over the years that it's not the face I make that gets me into trouble, but rather the face I don't."

Slim crossed his arms. "Like I told you, this case is a big damn deal. Eventually somebody'll need to be prosecuted, but this thing could drag on for years. They might not ever compile enough evidence to get a conviction against any of you, but are you prepared to make fighting this thing your new full-time job? Can you afford to pay lawyers for the thousands of man-hours it'll take to establish an adequate defense? Then even if a jury finds you all not guilty, you'll still be under a cloud of suspicion for the rest of your lives, which ain't gonna do any of your careers much good. It sure seems to me like somebody out there is trying to jam you up, and so far they're doing one hell of a job."

Chapter 21

Weston drove his rental car toward Chicago on the slush- and salt-covered interstate. "This road has more sodium than a corned beef sandwich."

"Was that supposed to be a joke?" Edwin asked from the passenger's seat.

"Not a very funny one, it would seem." Weston glanced in the rearview mirror and saw that Becky and Kate were asleep in the compact sedan's back seat. "It might've been a bit funnier if the only other person in the car who's awake wasn't a vegetarian, but only just."

"Thanks for driving me and Kate back to her condo."

"Sure thing...it didn't make sense for you two to rent a car as well just to drive back to the city, and since Slim agreed to drop off H.P., me and Becca will still get home in time to pick up the kiddos from her sister's."

"So how do you intend to exculpate us?" asked Edwin.

Weston smiled. "We still need to work some more on your transitions, but I've been thinking about that, Ed...what if you take the blame for everything, thereby clearing the rest of us in the process?"

Edwin frowned. "Not the solution I was hoping for, though if it came to that I would. Of the five of us, I feel I have the least to lose—except, of course, I don't want to lose Kate."

"In that case, tell me about the soup," said Weston. "You mentioned a large container of it, but I didn't see any in either fridge after we searched the house and went looking for something to eat in the kitchen. Anne thought you must've been mistaken when you brought it up earlier, but you my friend have the best memory of anyone I know...especially when it comes to food. So how much soup are we talking...like a quart?"

"No, it was a larger container than that."

"Like maybe the size of one of those four-liter wine jugs that you used to drink out at your telescope."

Edwin nodded. "Sure, about that size I'd say."

"And let me guess, the soup was red in color."

"That's right," said Edwin. "About a gallon of red soup that I didn't lift the lid off of to smell...you think that might've been the blood they found out in the barn?"

"I do. I think she'd been drawing her own blood, saving it up a pint at a time, which could explain why she seemed a little tipsier last night than the rest of us despite drinking less wine."

"I noticed that too...so you think Anne is still alive?"

"Yeah, I'd wager she secreted herself away somewhere in that house right after we heard her scream...someplace the cops haven't thought to look yet. The real question—at least for me—is why."

"That's the $64,000 question all right. She had so much going for her—state poet laureate, president of a successful company—why fake her own death and give all that up?"

Weston shook his head. "No, that part doesn't surprise me; the first time I met her, I could tell she was off. I mean, why go to all the trouble to implicate us in her death?"

Chapter 22

Slim drove past the interstate onramp. H.P. looked ahead at the barren road and then back at the busy interstate. "We're not taking the expressway back toward Chicago?"

"Nah, it's too crowded," answered Slim. "We'll bypass the city, and then hook up with I-57 downstate a ways."

"But wouldn't the expressway be better plowed?"

"More than likely, but it'll also be a damn sight busier…and it only takes one idget who doesn't know how to drive on icy roads to cause a pile up."

"But what if we hit an ice patch and end up on the side of the road? There won't be anyone around for miles to help us out of the ditch."

"This here truck has four-wheel drive," said Slim. "She was built for off-roading. We'll be okay."

H.P. glanced at the speedometer whose needle indicated decidedly less than interstate speeds. "In that case, could we go a bit faster?"

"Having four-wheel drive don't help you brake no quicker. See, this here's a shortcut. We'll shave off thirty miles as opposed to taking the interstate directly east to the city and then directly south, but the tradeoff is that in these conditions we'll have to drive about twenty miles slower than if we was on the expressway, so time-wise I guess you'd could call it a wash. The upside, though, is that going this a way there won't be no traffic and the scenery is a might prettier, so just sit back and enjoy the view. Don't worry, I'll get you home in time for your classes tomorrow."

"Sorry, Slim, I appreciate you driving out of your way to take me home...and for driving all the way up here in the first place."

"It ain't no big deal. If I wasn't doing this, I'd just be at home drinking beer and watching football."

H.P. stared out the window at the snow-covered trees and farmhouses. "You're right, it is pretty out here."

"Yep...driving through the country always makes me feel kind of peaceful like."

"I could certainly do with some of that feeling now."

Slim nodded. "Yeah, you seemed kinda broken up about Ms. Anne. Was you two close or something?"

"No, not really...but who knows—maybe we could've been one day. I guess I'll never get the chance to find out."

"That's a tough break, partner...gettin' sweet on a gal, then she gets killed and you get framed for her murder."

"Isn't that the story of some old country song?" H.P. asked.

"If it ain't, it ought to be. Want me to see if I can find some country music on the radio?"

"Would you mind if we listened to a football game instead?"

"10-4."

Chapter 23

The Pirate Hunter dove from the boat's deck just as the engine room exploded. Looking up from beneath the water's surface, the dark blues and purples of the twilight sky gave way to oranges and yellows from the fiery wreckage, like sunrise shot from a cannon. P.H. knew from experience that the air above would be superheated from the boiler's eruption and unbreathable for several moments. Had he been a younger guardsman, he would've attempted to swim underwater past the circumference of the explosion, but with experience comes wisdom. The better strategy was to conserve the air in his lungs and wait for the heat above to dissipate. Of course he still might not make it, but he had a better chance of holding his breath than outswimming the boiler's blast radius on open water, and maybe there'd be a nice piece of flotsam he could cling to waiting for him up top.

The conflagration above illuminated the murkiness below. The Pirate Hunter saw a figure swimming in the distance. As it moved toward him, he could make out its eyes…her eyes. She had beautiful green eyes and raven-colored hair. *Okay, so I must've taken a knock to the head as I jumped from the boat*, thought P.H. The mermaid swam circles around him, smiling coquettishly. He reached out to touch her, but his fingers only slipped between strands of her hair. She glided through the water with effortless grace.

P.H. became entranced as she encircled him. She seemed to be everywhere he looked, staring back at him with her come-hither gaze. Even so, part of his mind felt distracted; something was amiss. He needed to breathe—quite desperately, in fact. He swam to the surface and then gulped at the hot air that singed his throat. She popped her head above the water too; her wet hair perfectly framing those beguiling eyes. She smiled again and dived down below, flipping up her tail as she went. That's when the Pirate Hunter realized he'd jumped out of the frying pan and into the fire. His mermaid didn't have the flat tail of a dolphin, but the vertical caudal fin of a shark.

P.H. swam toward a piece of the boat's hull floating on its side. He pulled himself up as it bobbed in the choppy water. Just as he managed to crawl toward the dry part of the wreckage, the head of the shark broke through the water's surface and landed atop the wood that was submerged. It thrashed back and forth, gnashing its jagged teeth, and then opened wide its maw. The leviathan bit down on a board it mistook for P.H.'s leg. The plank snapped in two, and the shark slid back underwater.

The Pirate Hunter grabbed the board whose other end had splintered where it'd been bitten. He saw the dorsal fin circling back around. P.H. rose to his feet as best he could, grabbing the side of the hull for support. The shark's head shot out of the water, farther up the wreckage than it had before, where P.H.'s legs rested only a moment ago. He thrust the splintered board into the shark's eye like a harpoon. Still the shark propelled itself up toward P.H., and still he pushed the broken board down into its eye socket.

Finally, with its own blood flowing into its mouth, the shark retreated, leaving behind a crimson stream as it swam away.

****

H.P. sat up in bed and put his hand to his cheek, touching the drool that issued from the corner of his mouth. *Sometimes it's probably better that I don't have a sleeping partner*, he thought. H.P. took note of the time on the alarm clock and then returned his head to the pillow. He'd have to be on campus in a couple of hours.

Chapter 24

H.P. sat in his office chair, looking over the stack of papers on his desk at the young man sitting across from him.

"So my idea for the final story—"

"Wait," H.P. interrupted, "your idea? You mean you haven't started writing your last story for my class. The final stories are supposed to be 10-12 pages, and they're due on Friday."

"I know, but I've got four finals later this week, so when I need a break from studying for those I try to write, but then I just end up staring at a blank screen for like an hour; however, once I get started, I'm usually a very fast writer."

"Okay, though I'd advise that you start writing as soon as you leave here…or like three weeks ago."

The young man nodded. "Yeah, I read you. So my idea is that there are these twins—"

"Let me guess, identical…not fraternal."

"How did you know?"

"I can't tell you how many twin stories I've read over my years as a creative writing instructor, but I don't recall any of them ever involving fraternal twins." H.P. gestured for the young man to continue. "Anyway, pardon the interruption…please go on."

"So these twins are the sons of a brilliant painter and a famous opera singer, but get this—one of them is blind and the other deaf."

"Ah, very interesting." H.P. waited for a moment. "So…what's the conflict?"

"Well, uh, it must be very difficult to have a twin brother that you can't see…or hear, for that matter."

"Sure, I imagine that it would be, but I more meant what's the plot of your story."

"Right, that's why I'm here…I thought we could brainstorm a bit."

H.P. leaned back in his chair. "I'd be glad to chat through any ideas you might have, but you have to come up with the stories on your own…otherwise my creative writing course would just be a typing class."

"I did have one idea."

"Great, let's hear it."

"What do you think of this for a title: One if by Sound, Two if by See? It's 'see' with your eyes rather than 'sea' as in a body of water."

"I get it, but 'sound' doesn't really rhyme with 'land'…and 'sound' can also be a term for a body of water, so that's a little confusing too."

The young student lowered his head. "Oh, I didn't know that."

"Listen, don't get down about it…no one cares about the title so long as the story is good. Try this— instead of imagining your two characters in a blank space waiting for something to happen to them, think about some of your favorite stories and imagine how they might fit into the plots. I don't mean swap their names for the protagonists in books that you've read—but say you like heist stories…then imagine your twin brothers robbing a museum or maybe stopping a bank robbery. Or if you prefer sci-fi stories, then how would the bond between them make for an interesting space adventure? Have some fun with it, but most importantly start writing and stop staring at an empty screen. If you email me five good pages by Friday—that's just one page a day—then I'll give you a week-long extension to finish your story after finals are over."

The young man stood. "Thanks, that'd really be helpful."

"I'm glad, and don't worry about the title—call it Two Dudes in a Pickle, if you want...just be sure the dudes have an arc."

"You mean like a big boat to cross that sound?"

"Not an 'ark,' an arc...make sure something happens and that the brothers change somehow along the way."

The young man smiled. "I know what you mean." He opened the door to reveal the dean waiting out in the hallway.

The dean nodded to the young man as the student exited the small office. Then he entered and closed the door behind him. "I overheard some of the advice you gave him—good stuff, that."

"Thanks, I find that sometimes the students who seem to not be taking their work in my class seriously are really just suffering from paralysis by analysis. When they first write something, if what they see on the screen doesn't immediately live up to their expectations...well, it can be a difficult disappointment."

"Quite so." The dean sat down in the chair vacated by the student. "I hope what I'm about to tell you isn't also a difficult disappointment, but I have to place you on administrative leave for the time being."

H.P. sat up. "What...are you talking about?"

"This is coming directly from the chancellor."

"If that were so, she'd be here now."

The dean sighed. "I suppose that's true—be that as it may, she was very clear when I found her sitting in my office first thing this morning."

"I didn't realize the chancellor even knew who I was."

"If she didn't before, it's safe to assume that she does now. The chancellor informed me that you were party to—however obliquely—something indecorous over the weekend. I didn't ask for any details, and none were given, save that it involved the recently installed president of [company name redacted], which as you are aware has a longstanding relationship with this university. In fact, they were integral in helping us establish the new chem lab on the other side of campus."

H.P. nodded slowly. "I know the incident to which you're referring, but from what I understand the matter is still in the early stages of investigation. Whatever happened to innocent until proven guilty?"

"I've known you for a long time…I'm sure this—whatever it is—will be sorted out soon enough and your reputation will once more be above reproach as it always has been. The chancellor just feels that until such time, out of an abundance of caution—especially given recent situations in which the university has been made to navigate the fallout from the actions of faculty members who've gone, shall we say, rogue—that it would be better if you weren't seen on campus or interacting with students."

"Okay, in that case, I suppose I can review these final stories from home and just email the grades." H.P. reached for the stack of papers on his desk, but the dean stood and placed his hand on top of them.

"Think of this as an early winter break—with full pay and benefits, of course."

"But who will take over my grading?"

"We'll find someone...me perhaps. You were gracious enough to take over Fixer's classes when he...hmm, I suppose that's not the best example given the circumstances, but rest assured that everything is well in hand. Consider this a much-deserved sabbatical."

Chapter 25

Lance helped Weston set the dining room table as Becky checked the lasagnas in the oven and then returned to slicing garlic bread at the kitchen counter. Van and Ance played with blocks on the living room carpet. When the doorbell rang, Van stood up from the tower they'd built. "I'll get it."

Edwin, Kate, and H.P. stood on the front porch. H.P. entered with two bottles of wine. "How did your finals go, fresh-Van?"

"I'll know in a week or so when I get my grades," answered Van. "I think I did well enough to pass most of my classes."

"The first semester is always the hardest," Edwin said as he and Kate followed H.P. inside.

"Is that the term when you got your one and only B?" asked Weston from the dining room.

"Why they made an astronomy major take a dramaturgy course, I'll never understand."

Kate removed her scarf. "That's funny, my roommate freshman year was a theater major, and she had to take an astronomy course."

Edwin took off his coat. "Makes sense to me…star-crossed lovers are an enduring theme of the dramatic arts."

"Sounds to me like you should've gotten an A," said Van.

"I thought so. My final paper was on Caesar's Comet mentioned in Shakespeare's *The Tragedy of Julius Caesar*. I postulated that the comet seen in Rome during July of 44 BCE must've been the same comet recorded in China two months prior."

H.P. grinned. "Interesting…tell me, what did you think of Caesar's ghost making an appearance in the play?"

"Oh, I never actually read it," replied Edwin. "But there's a ghost in the play…that sounds rather silly."

Kate handed her coat to Edwin. "Your B is starting to sound well deserved."

Edwin handed the two coats he held to H.P. "What do you want me to do with these?"

"Put them wherever you're going to put yours," answered Edwin.

Van rolled his eyes. "Here, I'll take them…I can take the bottles too."

H.P. handed over the three coats. "You take these, and I'll take the wine into the dining room, but I'll be glad to pour you a glass later if it's okay with your mom."

"I'll ask her…after she's had a glass herself."

"Spoken like an erudite college student," said Kate.

The doorbell rang again. Van turned back toward the door as Weston entered from the dining room. "You go put those coats on the folding table in the laundry room, and I'll see who it is." Weston opened the front door to find Slim holding a punchbowl full of lettuce. "Great Caesar's Ghost salad!"

"Yeah, I asked Becky if I could bring something, and she suggested a salad. I figured two heads of lettuce are better than one, but I think I might've overdone it a bit…this is my first salad."

"Making or eating?"

****

Becky dished out the lasagna and Weston added a slice of garlic bread to each plate before passing it down the table.

Edwin eyed the large salad bowl. "Do you have any salad tongs?"

"For that size iceberg lettuce, I think you'd be better off using a couple of garden rakes," said Weston. "But I'll get you a pair in a minute."

Becky shook her head. "I'll get them. I made a vegetarian lasagna for Ed and anyone else who wants it, but it's still in the oven, so I'll grab the tongs when I go into the kitchen to plate it up."

"If you was to ask me, a meal with no meat ain't much different than a cheerleader with no pom-poms," said Slim. "Sure, she can shout out all them cheers, but folks still expect to see some shakin'."

"A sentiment as politically incorrect as it is grammatically incorrect," H.P. replied, "though I don't necessarily disagree with you."

Van looked across the table at H.P. "Now that I'm officially on winter break, my plans are to sleep in and watch TV. What are you going to do over your break?"

Weston passed a plate of lasagna and bread to H.P. "He should spend the time writing a sequel with me to our last book, but since he's sworn off his Pirate Hunter character, my Spinster is without a dance partner."

H.P. passed the plate down to Slim. "Van, I have every intention of also doing my share of sleeping and TV watching during my time off, though I already have a week's head start on you. On Monday I was placed on administrative leave because of what happened last weekend."

Becky handed another plate to Weston. "Yeah, a lot fewer cases have come my way this week from the state agencies my office liaises with, despite this typically being a very busy time of year for us."

"Isn't that a good thing?" Weston asked. "You're always saying how thin your office's resources are stretched."

"True, but I didn't go into social work for the soft schedule. I got in to help people."

"I've noticed something similar, though I thought perhaps it had to do with the holidays being fast upon us," said Kate. "Several companies who've been attempting to recruit me are in near-weekly contact, but I didn't hear from any of them this week."

Slim nodded. "I hate to say it, but that's how these things go when word starts to get out…especially with an investigation this high profile—and it'll only get worse from here on."

"So what do we do?" asked Becky.

"We figure out who killed Anne," answered H.P.

Weston took a sip of wine. "I like your thinking…except the part when you assumed she's actually dead."

H.P. turned to Weston. "You think she isn't?"

"I'm not convinced of it, no."

H.P. studied the marinara sauce on the plate in front of him. "But what about all the blood they found?"

Becky looked to her oldest son. "Vancy, would you mind taking your brother and sister into the kitchen to eat?"

"Aw, Mom," Lance protested. "I want to hear this."

"Do you, or do you want an extra helping of

dessert?"

"Pie and ice cream?" asked Lance.

"You drive a hard bargain, mister," said Becky. "Now go eat your dinner in the kitchen."

Weston waited to respond as Van helped Ance with her plate and Lance followed them into the kitchen. "Do you recall the soup that Ed thought he'd seen in the refrigerator, but that we didn't find when we regrouped in the kitchen after searching the house?"

"It's not at forefront of my recollections from last weekend," H.P. answered, "but yes, now that you mention it, I do recall…so your hypothesis is that the borscht or gazpacho or whatever Ed thought he saw earlier in the evening was actually Anne's blood, which she dumped in her barn-cum-studio prior to disappearing? But before you answer that question, answer this one: why?"

Weston set his wineglass down. "Well, like borscht and gazpacho, revenge is a dish best served cold…besides, it's almost winter—who's eating chilled soup these days. Someone had to have edited in the footage of Ed standing in the brush outside the barn from earlier this year; it seems reasonable to me that it was probably her, which would of course mean she knew that he was there the day her father died."

H.P. shook his head. "But why not report it to the police back then?"

"She likely surmised, and correctly so, that whatever Ed was up to, he wasn't alone," Weston answered. "However, if she had simply turned over the video to the cops, maybe they could've made charges stick against him—maybe not…but if instead she bided her time while she set her plan in motion and then invited us all into her web, catching us unawares, she could ensnare Ed's whole cohort."

H.P. crossed his arms. "Okay, but then where'd she go? The roads weren't plowed until the groundskeeper arrived. The police didn't find any secret rooms. The snow might've partially covered her tracks, but most of it had fallen by midnight before she went missing."

Weston swirled his wine. "I don't know where she went but, whether she staged her own murder or she was killed, we know something doesn't add up since there's no evidence of anyone leaving the grounds that night."

Slim cleared his throat. "As a general rule, I don't like to agree with Weston on account of him rarely knowing what the hell he's talking about, but I did touch base a couple of days ago with my friend who's on the job up there…now mind you, this is all second-hand information, but he told me that he spoke with one of the gals who worked the crime scene, and it seems the CSIs are as mystified as we are by that pool of blood found out in the barn."

"To collect that much blood, Anne must've been saving it up over time," said Becky. "Was some of the blood older than the rest?"

"No, nothing like that," Slim answered. "It's the pool itself that's got them scratching their heads. Say you stab or shoot somebody—usually what happens next is that the victim starts leaking red sauce as they writhe around in agony…maybe trying to get away so they don't get stabbed or shot again. Or, say it's a kill shot, and the victim dies right off, falling to the floor as the sauce drains out of 'em…well, then of course you've got to move the body if you want to get rid of it. Either way, it'll make an awful mess as all that sauce gets smeared about, but what the CSIs found out in that barn was almost a perfect red circle like the flag of Japan."

"As if it had been poured onto the floor," said Kate, "perhaps from a container intended to hold a large quantity of soup."

Slim pointed a finger at Kate and clicked his tongue. "Bingo."

"This is all very fascinating, and I fully understand that it directly impacts the possibility of my future incarceration," said Edwin, "but would you mind terribly if I popped into the kitchen to procure a piece of that vegetarian lasagna?"

Part Three

Chapter 26

Anne's executive assistant waited in her car down the road as the last police van drove off the Hedonia property. When the van disappeared in the distance, she keyed in a code on a cellphone app that disabled the security cameras and disarmed the house's alarm. Then she started her car and drove up the long driveway. She parked in front of the isolated ranch house, sent a text message, and then grabbed the satchel from the passenger's seat as she got out.

She climbed the front steps, ducked under the police tape hung across the door, and entered the house. Inside she found rooms cordoned off with more tape and covered by evidence markers. She made her way to the cellar door and descended the stairs. She approached the large wine cask in the darkened corner and knocked three times on the head of the horizontal barrel—then twice more.

The barrel head turned, slowly unscrewing from the chime hoop. When the end twisted off, Anne emerged from the barrel covered in granola bar wrappers and other detritus. "Jesus, it's good to be out of there."

"I can't believe you lasted a whole week in that thing. I figured the cops would've left after a couple of days."

"I'd hoped they would, but day after day I heard new voices down here…though by the end of the week, some of those might've been coming from inside my head." Anne leaned on her assistant for support as she strained to stand up straight, her joints popping in protest. "That feels both terrific and terrible."

"If not for your yoga exercises, I doubt you'd be capable of standing at all." The executive assistant crouched down to poke her head inside the cask. "It's warm in there."

"Surrounding that compartment is a four-inch layer of fermenting wine, which gives off about the same heat as my body temperature."

"So you wouldn't show up on a thermal scan."

"Correct, which is also why I didn't take a phone in with me in case the cops swept for electronics or cell signals—just a handful of glow sticks and a stack of paperbacks to pass the time. It was nice to get caught up on my sleep, though I had this recurring dream that I was trapped inside a casket."

"You really thought of everything." The assistant took the empty water bottles and wrappers from inside the compartment and put them in her satchel.

"We'll see, but right now I need your help getting up the stairs. The first thing I'm going to do is take a long shower."

The assistant shook her head. "Sorry, no. You made me promise to text the moderator the moment I knew the house was clear and that you'd be rising from the dead. It seems he's had a difficult week allaying the concerns of the council since news broke of your disappearance and presumed demise, despite his assurances that reports of your death were greatly exaggerated. A quick hello from you would go a long way to calm a lot of nerves. By now, he and most of the council are likely waiting for you in the virtual meeting room."

Chapter 27

"I'm certain I speak for all of us when I tell you how pleased we are that you're still alive," said the moderator. "How does it feel to be back among the living?"

"Liberating," Anne answered from inside her assistant's car parked along a deserted country road. "I suspect reports of my disappearance caused most Illinoisians to ask, 'We had a poet laureate?' Though, unlike other dead artists, I'll have the unique opportunity to see if my work actually becomes more popular after my death."

"We're all very impressed with your disappearing act," said a stern woman's voice from Anne's laptop, "but now that you've successfully steered your father's company in an advantageous direction for us and effectively neutralized the unlikely group that foiled our previous projects, we're all anxious to know what we can expect for the next part of your plan?"

"As some of you are aware, I've had an underground lab working on a formula for a variant of tyramine."

"The chemical in alcohol and cheese that causes migraines in some people?" asked the stern woman.

"That's correct," answered Anne. "As a long-time sufferer of migraines myself, I know how debilitating they can be."

"Then wouldn't it make more sense for this

laboratory to be working on a cure?" asked a male voice.

"I have another lab working on that—in tandem...and both formulas are nearly complete."

"To what end?" asked the man.

"The variant, which I've named Tyrantmind, triggers migraines in all people—not just migraineurs—who stare at the screens of digital devices for more than a few minutes."

An uncommon moment of silence from the council followed Anne's statement. Finally, the moderator spoke up. "I don't get it."

Anne sighed. "When I first inquired if such a compound could be created, I was assured—after some preliminary research—that indeed it could. However, I won't waste your time by pretending that I understand the neuroscience behind it all...suffice it to say, Tyrantmind facilitates a chain reaction that results in selective cerebral dilation of the cranial vessels found in the occipital cortex, which when coupled with the eyestrain brought on by the blue lights emitted from digital screens results in an ocular migraine that intensifies the longer the exposure. In addition to severe headaches, the symptoms range from nausea to temporary loss of vision."

"No, I mean...I don't get how that benefits us?"

Anne chuckled. "Are you kidding? In our screen-obsessed society, you don't think the masses would pay through the nose to counteract migraines brought on by looking at their cellphones and computers?"

"Okay," said the stern woman, "that's interesting, but how do we get the...Tyrantmind to the, uh, consumer?"

"Water. Unless you know what to look for, the

compound is nearly undetectable since its molecular structure resembles the additives used to fluoridate drinking water."

"Very clever," complimented a male voice. "So then we monetize this stratagem of yours by selling the cure that you have under development."

"That's right," Anne replied.

"And how much do we stand to profit?" the stern woman asked.

"If the predictive models I've seen are to be believed, upwards of two and a half billion dollars a quarter. How does that sound?"

"Like almost enough." The stern woman laughed...then other council members joined in her laughter.

Chapter 28

Slim scanned the horizon with his binoculars from the passenger's seat of Weston's rental car. "My buddy told me the CSIs cleared out earlier today…and I don't see no vehicles in the driveway or on the property."

"I know it's a large house," said H.P. from the backseat, "but did they really need a whole week to search it?"

Slim lowered his binoculars. "Nope, but the investigators used the house as sort of a base of operations while they waited for the snow to melt so they could comb the grounds."

"Couldn't they use one of those thermal thingamabobs to look for something under the snow?" asked Weston.

"A frozen body is the same temperature as the frozen ground," answered Slim. "And it's a mighty big property to cover, even for a search party outfitted with snowshoes and pokey sticks."

"I take it they didn't find anything?" Edwin asked from the backseat.

Slim shook his head. "No, they were diligent about searching every day as the snow melted outta concern that coyotes or anything else roaming around out here might drag off a thawing body, but all they found were downed tree limbs from the storm."

Weston sighed. "So our plan is to sneak into the

house and see if we can find something a whole team of crime scene investigators couldn't find during all of last week?"

"I never said it was a good plan," replied Slim. "In fact, I don't believe it even was my plan. I'm just along for the ride in what you might call an advisory capacity."

"Do you think there's any chance the cops reset the alarm on the house when they left?" asked H.P.

Slim nodded. "In all likelihood they did, but I can help with that…my buddy also gave me the alarm code."

"That's quite a friend," said Weston.

Slim smiled. "Yeah, some friends actually help you instead of always asking for help, though I did save his skin once in a shootout."

"Won't the police be notified by the alarm company that the code has been entered and the alarm disabled?" asked Edwin.

"There's a good chance of that," Slim answered, "which is why it's better that we're here the same day the team pulled up stakes. Decampment for an operation this size usually involves some level of confusion. I figure if the local boys in blue do get such a notification from the alarm company, whoever takes the call down at the station might assume somebody forgot something and went on back for it…but hell, I could be wrong, so it'd probably be best if we do this thing on the quick."

Weston started up the compact sedan, and the engine anemically sputtered to life. "I sure hope we don't have to make a fast getaway in this car."

Chapter 29

Slim shined his flashlight on the wooden stairs. "Okay, Weston, you wanted to start with the cellar, so lead the way."

Weston took point with his LED lantern as the other three followed him down the stairs. "I thought this wine cellar was creepy at night during a storm when we were looking for a possible intruder or a dead body, but I've got to say—even in the middle of the day, being down here still gives me the creeps. H.P., I'll never understand how you found the nerve to put the moves on Anne in this cellar."

H.P. tugged on a small chain hanging from an Edison socket affixed to the ceiling. The uncovered bulb illuminated the area around them. "It's not so bad with the lights on."

Slim looked around in awe. "There's enough wine here to stock a liquor store."

"Anne told us her father liked to entertain," said Edwin.

"Who?" asked Weston. "All the attendees of a bacchanalia?"

H.P. stopped in front of the large wine cask. "That's where we had our kiss."

Weston put a hand on his shoulder. "I think it's time to get over her...she's trying to frame us for murder."

"We don't know that for certain," said H.P.

"So you bent her over this barrel and laid one on her?" asked Weston. "I've got to tell you, picturing that doesn't do much to make being down here any less creepy. I hope you kept your hands out of the bunghole."

"It wasn't like that—a nice kiss...the first of many, I'd hoped."

Weston knocked on the cask and heard liquid slosh within. "It's warm to the touch for being in a basement that's so cool."

H.P. placed a hand on the wooden staves. "Wine gives off heat during fermentation. Red wines can reach temperatures of about 90 degrees."

"Is that right?" Weston pulled the bung from the cask's hole. "I say we uncork this wine."

"Are you planning to take some home with you?" asked Edwin.

Weston shook his head. "No, but I find it curious that with all these bottles of wine down here they would bother to...what'd you call it, H.P.—you know, winemaking?"

"It's called vinification," H.P. answered, "and now that you mention it, I think it rather odd that they have only the one cask. You can't just take wine that's fermenting in a barrel such as this and serve it up. You'd have to clarify it first, which would require filtration equipment. It'd be something of a hassle to do all that for a single cask...even one as large as this."

Weston unfolded his pocketknife and poked it down into the bunghole. "This big barrel puts me in mind of my book *Smuggling Spinster*, in which she snuck refugees hidden inside of oil drums to freedom." The knife's handle had barely gotten wet when the blade's tip hit something solid.

Slim approached the cask with the beam of his flashlight shining into the bunghole. "I think this here barrel bears closer inspection."

Chapter 30

Anne's executive assistant parked in front of a trailer in a small clearing off a dirt road. "This looks more like the foreman's office at a construction site—not some high-tech lab."

"That's the point," Anne replied from the passenger's seat. "If it looked like a modular section of a moon base, then every inquisitive hunter and woodsman would try to peek in the windows."

The two exited the car and climbed the rickety front steps. Inside an elderly man sat at a modest desk, drinking coffee. "Can I help you?"

"I'm a courier sent by my client to pick up a package," said Anne's assistant.

The elderly man turned to Anne. "And who's she...your bodyguard?"

Anne smiled. "Something like that."

He eyed the two skeptically and then pulled out a fingerprint scanner from a desk drawer. "I need you both to take turns pressing your right index finger and thumb against the little screen here, so that I can bring up the order and verify that the transaction has cleared."

Anne and her assistant did as instructed. The elderly man typed on his outmoded computer, hunting and pecking his way across the clunky keyboard. Satisfied with what his monitor revealed, he looked up at the pair. "Okay, you're all set...just go on back to the lab."

Anne's assistant pointed to a shabby wood door leading to the rear two-thirds of the trailer. "Through that door?"

"Yep, there's a small waiting area before you enter the cleanroom. One of the lab techs will be with you in a moment."

The elderly man buzzed them in. Anne and her assistant opened the door to a bright and modern, albeit narrow, lab with two technicians working on the other side of a plexiglass partition. The tech closest to the door nodded at them, picked up a case from the counter, and slid open the door to the tiny waiting room.

"Here's your product." The young laboratorian pulled the hood back from his cleanroom suit, careful not to touch anything in the small space. "We just finished synthesizing it yesterday."

Anne accepted the case and flipped up its catches. Inside were two transparent canisters containing fine, white crystals. "It looks like salt."

"And it'll dissolve like salt in liquid, though I wouldn't recommend using it on your next margarita. I know I communicated this to you in my emails, but now that I'm meeting you in person, I feel I should reiterate that without proper testing we don't know this compound's degree of efficacy. It may only cause headaches in human subjects who ingest it, or it could cause permanent blindness. The brain is an intricate organ to say the least, making the impact of untested toxins capable of permeating the blood-brain barrier difficult to predict."

"I appreciate you raising your concerns to me." Anne closed the case. "Rest assured that I have human test subjects in mind as well as another lab working on an antidote based on the research you've sent me these past few months."

"That's good to know," said the laboratorian. "I'll require several weeks' notice should you need any more product."

"I'll keep that in mind." Anne reopened the door to the front office. "We'll let you get back to work now."

Anne waved at the elderly man behind the desk as she and her assistant exited the trailer. The assistant turned to Anne as they descended the front steps. "Now I suppose you want me to drive you to the other lab that's probably also in the middle of nowhere."

"There is no other lab."

Chapter 31

Weston pushed the shopping cart as Ance sat in the child's seat, playing with the drawstring hanging from his hooded sweatshirt. "What's wrong with the toy robots we got for Lance?"

"Nothing." Becky moved behind Weston to let another cart in the crowded sporting-goods aisle pass in the opposite direction. "That's one thing I miss about the pandemic—everybody had to swim in the same direction."

"To quote Thomas Paine: When men yield up the privilege to push carts how they please, the last shadow of liberty quits the horizon."

"I think you're paraphrasing."

"No, I'm pretty sure that's a direct quote." Weston examined the price tag on a catcher's mitt. "Those robots were expensive."

"I know they were expensive. I'm the one who went to three different stores to find them all."

"So then why are we still shopping for Christmas gifts for Lance?"

"He's a sixth grader now. You know what that means—presents aren't the only thing he'll be getting soon…puberty."

"Yeah, I've heard of it, but he asked for those robots."

"Right, but I suspect in a couple of months he won't

have any interest in them anymore."

Weston picked up a football. "Maybe, but he's expressed no interest in any of this stuff either."

"Well, you were his age once...what do boys want when they lose interest in their toys?"

"Stuff that their mothers shouldn't pick out for them."

Becky sighed. "Let's go look at backpacks...maybe he'd like something a little more mature than the superhero one he uses for school."

"How about a briefcase then?"

"That's a really helpful suggestion; I'm so glad you made it home in time to come shopping with me." Becky noticed the crowd thinning out as they navigated away from the toys and sporting goods departments. "So did you find anything interesting at the house?"

"There's a large wine cask in the cellar with a secret compartment that Anne could've hidden in."

"For a whole week while the cops were there?" asked Becky.

"It definitely smelled like someone had been in there recently and for a substantial amount of time."

"Wow, so she's committed to her cause...whatever that is. Is Slim going to report it?"

"How would that work? We didn't exactly have permission to be there, though we did leave the end of the cask off, so I'm sure the police will discover it sooner or later and hopefully reach the same conclusion that we did."

"I hope so too." Becky shook her head. "That duplicitous harpy went to a lot of effort to set us up; I still can't get over the way she lied to our faces...lied to H.P. If the cops eventually realize that we didn't have any involvement in her disappearance, do you think she'll come after us?"

"Possibly, but now we have the advantage."

"And what's that?"

"She doesn't know that we know she's still alive."

"That doesn't sound like much of an advantage…more like just enough information to get us into worse trouble." Becky tickled Ance under the chin. "It's almost this little girl's bedtime, and I don't want to think anymore tonight about my little boy growing up. If tomorrow at work is as slow as all of last week was, then I'll have plenty of time to order him something online at my office."

"Give me liberty or give me delivery."

"Okay, I'm positive Thomas Paine didn't say that."

Chapter 32

Anne and her executive assistant followed Kate, Edwin, and H.P. into the parking lot of a pizza parlor. The assistant parked near the far end of the small lot as Kate pulled into a spot near the entrance. Anne turned to then see Weston and Becky drive into the lot. "I was disappointed when we tailed Edwin out of the city earlier today, but I think this is going to work out better than I could've anticipated."

The assistant watched as Weston parked next to Kate's car. After quick hellos out in the cold, the five entered the restaurant together. "These guys sure like to hang out a lot."

"They seem to be as thick as thieves, which so far has worked in our favor."

"So how do you want to do this? Should we try to sneak in the back door and spike their waterglasses in the kitchen?"

Anne eyed her assistant's dark pants and white blouse. "I think a more direct approach is in order." Anne pulled a bottle of wine and a corkscrew from a satchel on the backseat. "Here, you open this, and I'll measure out some of the Tyrantmind." The bottle uncorked and the case opened, Anne poured a minute amount of the compound into the wine. "This seems like the kind of place that sells wine by the carafe. Find an empty one or some glasses to pour the wine into. Then walk right up to their table like you're a waitress and inform them that it's compliments of the house."

****

The waitress sat the quintet at a corner booth in the dimly lit restaurant. "Would you like to get started with some drinks?"

"We're expecting one more, but he should be along soon, so I think we can go ahead and order," answered Weston. "We'll have two large pizzas—one garbage, the other vegetarian—the appetizer sampler, a family-size house salad in case my doctor should happen to see me here, and a carafe of red wine. And please tell Ramone that Becky says 'hey.' "

The waitress smiled. "I'll get that order into the kitchen and be back in a moment with your wine."

"So what did Slim want to discuss?" asked H.P.

"He wouldn't say over the phone," Weston replied, "but when I mentioned that Ed and Kate were staying with you for a few days to use your backyard for some stargazing, he suggested we all meet up for pizza, so I assume it's good news."

Kate nodded. "That makes sense—no one breaks bad news over pizza."

"I'm curious," said Edwin. "Exactly what sorts of food are good for breaking bad news?"

"Lobster and crème brulée, I imagine," answered Becky. "They're both extravagant and require crushing."

The assistant approached the booth and set a carafe of wine on the table. "Here—this is for you."

"That was fast," H.P. said. "Thanks."

"Enjoy."

"We might enjoy it a bit more if we had glasses too." Weston looked up from the table, but she was already gone.

Slim approached from the opposite direction. "Howdy y'all."

"Hello, young man." Edwin slid closer to Kate in the large horseshoe booth to make room for Slim on the end.

The waitress arrived as Slim sat down. She set out five wineglasses and a carafe, then noticed the carafe already on the table.

"The other waitress brought it over," said Becky.

"You can leave that one too," added Weston. "I'm sure we would've ended up ordering a second carafe anyhow."

"Oh…okay." The waitress turned to Slim. "Should I bring another glass for you?"

"Nah, I'll just have a beer when you get a chance."

"So what news do you have for us?" Kate asked as the slightly confused waitress left the table.

"Good news," answered Slim.

"I'm conducting a poll," Edwin said. "What sort of food would you've suggested we eat if you'd had bad news to share?"

Slim rubbed his chin. "I dunno…maybe something crunchy like pork rinds or extra-crispy catfish."

Becky smiled. "That's extravagant in these parts."

Slim shook his head. "Uh, anyways—my cop buddy called earlier today to tell me that their investigation is transitioning to a missing-persons focus, so it looks like you all might be off the hook…at least for the time being."

"Why the change?" asked Weston.

"The CSIs went back out to the house this morning after getting a report that the alarm had been disabled yesterday—twice…and they found that barrel with its end twisted off."

H.P. began filling the wineglasses. "The alarm had been shut off twice?"

Slim nodded. "Yep, according to the alarm company, once in the morning through their app and then again around noon when we entered the code on the keypad by the door."

"Did they find anything else interesting aside from the compartment in the cask?" asked Edwin.

"Nope, but they did find something missing. I guess they'd done a pretty thorough inventory of all them wine bottles in that cellar, looking for anomalous prints as they went. Since they figured somebody had clearly been down there, they double checked their inventory and discovered that one of the bottles was missing."

****

All that remained on the table were empty plates, a minimally eaten bowl of salad, and a mostly finished carafe. The waitress stopped by to check in. "Can I box up this salad for you and bring you all another carafe?"

Weston sighed. "I guess we'll take the salad, though I suspect instead of you throwing it away here, we'll just end up throwing it away at home in a few days. Anybody want more wine?"

Kate shook her head. "No, I'm good."

"I'd have another glass if it tasted like that first carafe," H.P. said, "but the second left something to be desired."

Becky nodded. "I agree, that first carafe was excellent, but the second disappointing by comparison. Did you get in a new wine?"

"No," answered the waitress. "We've still got the same three we've always had: our house red, our house white, and our rosé—which between us is a blend of the red and white."

"Just the check then," said Weston. "Thanks."

"Sure thing, I'll be right back." The waitress left the table with the large salad bowl.

Edwin finished off his glass of wine. "H.P., I'm not the wine connoisseur that you are, but I agree that, despite being the same color, that carafe the other waitress brought was far superior."

"It tasted familiar too," added Kate, "like I'd had it recently."

H.P. studied his empty wineglass. "It reminded me of the pinot noir we had at Anne's last weekend."

During the ruminative moment that followed H.P.'s remark, Becky scanned the restaurant. "You know, I don't see that other waitress anywhere…now that I think of it, I haven't seen her since she dropped off the wine."

"Maybe her shift was ending when she brought over the wine," said Weston, "which might explain why she seemed somewhat out of sorts, since probably all she wanted to do was go home after a long day of waiting tables."

"Yeah…maybe," Becky replied. "I'll ask our waitress when she gets back."

Slim clapped his hands together as if giving himself a high five. "Yes!"

"What's the rumpus?" asked Weston.

"Chicago's playing Green Bay on Monday Night Football. I've got ten bucks riding on the Bears, and they just scored another touchdown."

Weston craned his neck to see the television near the pick-up window in the lobby, then instantly put his hand to his mouth and lurched forward.

"Are you okay?" asked Becky.

"I think so...I suddenly felt nauseous for some reason."

"Probably indigestion brought on by a middle-aged man eating too many pepperonis," said Edwin. "You're not as young as I used to be."

"It could also be a symptom of appendicitis," Kate warned.

Weston sat up again. "Believe me, I know. I've already had my appendix out."

H.P. checked the Bear's score on his smartphone and a moment later set his phone on the table. "Argh."

Noticing the Bear's logo on the phone's screen, Slim asked, "You didn't bet against the Bears, did you?"

H.P. covered his eyes with his hand, rubbing his temples with his thumb and middle finger. "No, I just got a splitting headache."

Becky slid a waterglass toward him. "Here, drink some water."

H.P. lowered his hand slowly, revealing a distraught expression. "I...can't see anything."

Slim took note of the five wineglasses on the table and then his own empty bottle of beer. He pulled his cellphone from his pocket and dialed 9-1-1. "This is Slim. We need some EMTs over here at the pizzeria along the Vermilion River—pronto."

Chapter 33

Slim stood in the corridor outside of a small recovery ward, waiting to talk with the attending physician after she finished her morning rounds. When she emerged from the room, Slim approached. "How are they doing, Doc?"

"Fine, Officer...a good night's rest—or what passes for one in a hospital—seems to have been just the tonic they needed."

"So they're good to go?"

"I don't think they need to be quarantined any longer, though I'd like to run some more tests and keep them the full twenty-four hours for observation, but they'll be ready to leave by tonight." She quickly referred to the chart on her aluminum clipboard. "The two females had the mildest cases, each presenting with headaches that abated after taking acetaminophen. The large fellow complained of abdominal distress, but his gut settled down when we fed him some agar gelatin. It says here that he ate a prodigious amount...the overnight nurse logged strawberry as his favorite flavor."

Slim crossed his arms. "What about the other two?"

"After reviewing their medical histories with this hospital, I'm in favor of having a full-time forensic toxicologist on staff to meet their potential future needs. Mr. Payley's symptoms subsided once we acquiesced to his seemingly irrational demand that the television be

111

removed from the room, which at first the orderlies interpreted as a reaction to the reversals of the Bear's performance last night. Surmising that blue lights were somehow affecting their conditions, I had the overhead LEDs turned off and shaded lamps with conventional bulbs brought in—soon after H.P.'s eyesight fully returned…he was even able to sign an autograph for me."

"So what about their tox report?"

"The ten-panel urine analysis we administered came back negative for each of them, so we can rule out substances associated with the most common illicit drugs; however, we won't get the results from the full tox screen of their blood samples for several days yet."

"When can I see them?" asked Slim.

"They're all awake, so you can go in now if you like—just keep your mobile phone in your pocket."

"You bet…one last question—you're a fan of the Pirate Hunter?"

"The swagger of a swashbuckler, and the heart of a saint…what's not to adore?"

Slim did his best to suppress an it-takes-all-kinds expression. "Thanks, Doc." As the physician walked up the corridor to continue her morning chores, Slim entered the recovery ward and waved to the five patients convalescing in bed. "Don't you all look a sight better than you did last night when we first got here?"

"Seeing your ugly mug this early in the morning makes me wish I'd been the one stricken by hysterical blindness," said Weston.

H.P. shook his head. "It wasn't hysterical blindness…my loss of vision merely occasioned a brief bout of what some might characterize as mild hysteria."

Weston rolled his eyes. "I haven't experienced so much wailing since the last time I read *Moby Dick*."

"Young man, did you perchance notice a breakfast trolley out in the hallway?" asked Edwin. "I put in a request last night for some more of that delicious vegan Jell-O."

Becky sighed. "Did anyone tell you when we'd be getting released?"

"We'd be glad to pay extra for an early checkout," added Kate.

Slim smiled. "It sounds like unless they find something else wrong with y'all that they'll cut you loose later on today, so hang in there."

"You got any leads on that waitress?" asked Weston.

Slim nodded. "After I left here, I went back to the restaurant to review their surveillance video. Their cameras are in definite need of an upgrade."

"Lo-def, black-and-white?" asked H.P.

"Yep," answered Slim. "Got the gal coming in the front door...mid-twenties, average height, hair dark in color. Then I got her going back out to the parking lot a few minutes later. She gets into a sedan...late-model, midsize, dark in color."

"Anybody in the car?" asked Becky.

"Yeah, there's a blurry figure in the passenger's seat, so maybe it's Ms. Hedonia...or anybody else who also happens to have a torso."

"That's not much to go on," said Kate.

"No, it ain't, but I'm fixin' to head back over there now that the sun's up and see if I can't find some—"

"Clues?" interrupted Edwin.

"We in the law enforcement community don't much care for that term, but I guess that's about right."

Chapter 34

Slim stepped eight yellow lines over from the end of the back row in the parking lot to where he remembered the car in question being parked the night before on the video. Standing in the middle of the space, he looked around. He saw litter and oil spots.

Slim walked to the front door of the pizza parlor and peered in the window. The restaurant workers wouldn't arrive for another couple of hours. He ambled around to the back of the building and found a smokers' pole for the workers who smoked to dispose of their cigarette butts. He cast his eyes over the wide gravel path that led down to the river and took note of all the butts amid the rocks. *When I smoked as a younger man,* Slim thought, *half the fun was flicking away your butt when you'd finished your square.*

A man with a fishing pole ascended the path from the water's edge. He looked up at Slim and nodded. "Morning."

"Howdy." Slim saw his breath as he spoke. "You catch anything when it's this cold?"

"Nah, but it's peaceful, you know. Did catch a glimpse of a lady on the other side of the river about a half hour ago."

"That's peculiar this time of day. She wasn't in distress, was she?"

The man shook his head as he approached. "No—

waved at me real friendly like."

"This an elderly lady with blonde hair…maybe a little heavyset?"

"Nope, younger gal with dark hair—athletic looking…had on what appeared to be climbing gear, at least so far as I could tell from the opposite bank."

"Climbing gear?" Slim scanned the horizon. "There ain't a mountain around here for—" He stopped midsentence when his gaze fell upon a water tower downriver that stood above the treetops.

****

Anne emerged with an empty canister from the manhole set in the top of the spherical water tower. "That ought to do it."

"You don't want to use the other one too?" asked her assistant as she helped her boss back onto the sphere's metal surface.

"No, we might need the other half sooner rather than later. Besides, we don't know how much damage this much will do."

"That's a good point, and I suppose the more we use, the easier it'd be to detect."

Anne sat up with her legs dangling down into the manhole. "That's right—even though a cursory analysis would most likely identify this compound as a fluoridization agent, it could make someone curious as to why there's suddenly so much more of it in the water supply."

"Okay, let's seal up this hatch so that we can get off this thing. I'm scared of heights."

Anne gave her assistant a puzzled expression. "I didn't know that. Why didn't you say so before we climbed all the way up here?"

"Because I believe in your cause."

****

Slim parked his pickup along the access road leading to the Reichenbach hydroelectric dam. Near the riverbank between the dam and the water treatment plant stood an enormous water tower that supplied the entire town. He got out of his truck with his binoculars and looked up. The tower cast a long shadow. He noticed two dangling lines hanging from the far side of the tower.

Slim walked along the bank of the river to the base of the tower, then he continued around the tower's perimeter to the opposite side and discovered that the two lines were a rope ladder hanging from the metal ladder running down the side of the large sphere. He tugged on the ladder. Feeling that it was securely attached, he began to climb.

****

Anne began her descent on the ladder that started at an almost horizontal angle near the top of the tower's sphere. As she climbed down to the point where she was nearly vertical, she spotted Slim climbing up the rope ladder. She quickly reascended the ladder and raced to her assistant, who was packing up her satchel near the hatch covering the manhole. "That cop is coming up."

"The one from the pizza place last night?" asked the assistant. "The one you told me pals around with the others."

"Yes, it looks like him."

"How far up is he? Can we climb down and detach the rope ladder?"

"I don't think we have time for that; he's nearly to the metal ladder."

"So what should we do?"

Anne studied the sturdy hinge of the hatch and took a climbing rope from her backpack. "We'll tie a line here and rappel down the other side."

"I did mention that I'm afraid of heights, right?"

"Your choices at this point are rappel, jump, or jail. You've got on your harness. I'll run the line through it, and you'll start rappelling like I showed you before."

"Oh…okay."

Anne fed the rope through the loops of her assistant's climbing harness. "I'll try to slow his ascent by dropping some of the tools in my pack on him, then I'll follow you down once I see that you're well on your way."

"Even with gravity on our side, if he's almost to the metal ladder, I doubt we can get down before he gets up here."

Anne tied a clove hitch knot with the end of the climbing rope around the hatch's steel hinge. "We don't have to…he's a cop—it's not like he's going to get up here and then untie this knot so that we fall to our deaths. All he can do is climb back down after us on our line or the rope ladder. Either way, we'll have a head start and reach the ground long before him."

Anne's assistant looked to her boss, the blustering wind blowing the hair from her face.

"You've got this—even if we land hard, from this side we'll land in the water, in which case we can make our escape down the spillway just before the dam. No one would be crazy enough to follow us then."

The assistant smiled. "That's true."

"You bet it is—now go!"

As her assistant began to descend, Anne got back onto the ladder and climbed down to where she could once again see Slim. "You're better than halfway there, cowboy."

Slim tilted his head to look up at Anne. "Ma'am, I'd be glad to go back down, if you'd be so kind as to accompany me."

"No, I'm going to keep playing hard to get, but I suspect I'll see you on terra firma soon enough." Anne climbed back up to the top of the tower, opened the hatch, untied the rope from the hinge, and sealed herself inside the manhole, shutting out the screams of her falling assistant.

Chapter 35

Slim entered the recovery ward as quietly as an opossum while the quintet gathered their things to leave. Weston noticed him as he took a seat. "Why the long face, buddy?"

"It's been one of those days." Slim stretched his legs out in front of him.

"Want to tell us about it?" asked Becky.

"I suppose somebody should," replied Slim. "I spent the afternoon helping with a recovery effort down at the dam."

"Recovering what?" asked Edwin.

"The body of Anne Hedonia," Slim answered. "I got a tip that she was seen along the river with climbing gear. Sure enough I discovered that she'd scaled the town's water tower over by the dam, presumably to dose the local water supply with whatever she slipped you all last night. Anyway, she spotted me as I climbed up the tower after her, so she tied a rope at the top to rappel down the other side, but I guess in her haste to make an escape, she didn't tie the knot too good, and it come undone. She fell to her death. The scream was something awful. Her body landed in the river, and the current pulled her into the reservoir just before the dam. The line she was trailing got sucked through the intake grate, then got all twisted up in the turbine, which eventually pulled her through the grate too. As you might imagine, what came out in the waterway below the dam was a grisly mess."

Kate shook her head. "That's ghastly."

Becky nodded in agreement. "Absolutely horrifying."

"What are you talking about?" asked Weston. "This is the best dam news I've ever heard—ding dong, the witch is dead." Becky tilted her head toward H.P., and Weston glanced at his friend who had his feet over the side of the bed with one shoe on as he held the other in his hands. "I didn't mean to call her a witch. She had some redeeming qualities…great taste in wine."

H.P. looked up from his shoe. "Yeah, she was quite an oenophile. I know it sounds crazy, but I liked her—then I was told she died…then that she might still be alive. I just hoped our paths might cross again, and she'd explain how this whole thing was all a misunderstanding."

"Nobody can blame you for wanting to see the best in someone," said Becky.

"So was she successful in poisoning the water supply?" Edwin asked, oblivious to the emotions in the room.

Slim shook his head. "No, the techs at the water treatment facility took a sample and didn't find any foreign particulates that caused them concern, but they flushed the water up in the tower just to be safe. The town's water pressure might be a little low for the next couple of days, but otherwise everything's copacetic in that regard. I guess I spooked her before she could finish what she climbed up there to do."

"I know this isn't exactly a happy ending," said Weston, "but at least we don't have to worry about looking over our shoulders anymore."

Kate frowned. "That's the second time in two days I've heard that same sentiment expressed."

Chapter 36

Weston sat in his recliner reading a movie magazine as Becky folded laundry on the couch. "It's kind of nice having the television off for a change."

"Tell that to the boys," replied Weston. "They've sequestered themselves in their rooms to view their various screened devices. Depending on how long our symptoms last, we might not see them for the rest of winter break."

"The light in the laundry room is an LED, and it didn't bother me."

"I checked my phone a little while ago and got a slight headache, but not bad. I suppose we could let them watch TV down here."

"You did hear me when I mentioned that it was nice having a bit of peace and quiet in our own home, right?"

"We'll let them watch TV tomorrow." He leaned back in the recliner and returned his attention to the magazine.

"You just spent most of the day sitting in bed at the hospital, so you come home and all you want to do is sit some more."

"I'm taking a pause for the cause."

"You've been doing a lot of cause pausing lately."

"It's a side effect of aging, I'm afraid."

She threw a sock at his magazine. "I don't ever remember seeing you read a magazine. Do you have a subscription I don't know about?"

"Nah, these days I mostly read magazines on my tablet, but I filched this one from the hospital because it has a fascinating article on stuntmen and the history of the Texas Switch."

She stacked Ance's little folded shirts in the basket, but the column of laundry toppled over. "Slim told us that fake waitress the restaurant had on video came in through the front door."

"Yeah, probably just some random person Anne paid to deliver the dosed wine so that she could keep from being seen."

"Right, but Slim also told us that there was a blurry figure caught on video sitting in the passenger's seat of the car the phony waitress got into."

He lowered his magazine. "So?"

"So if she was just some rando that Anne gave fifty bucks to or whatever for her to drop off the wine, isn't it more likely that Anne would've been the one driving?"

"Where are you going with this?"

"Couldn't the waitress have been the person Slim saw fall from the water tower? He did say that she started to climb down the other side as he finished climbing up…and it's not like he could've seen her face all that well from the top of the tower when she fell into the water. The cops certainly couldn't have IDed her after she came out through the dam—they just assumed it was Anne based on what Slim had told them."

"Because he saw her," said Weston.

"Right, at the top of the tower looking down at him, but maybe there was someone else up there that he didn't see…like the phony waitress who was driving the car the two left the restaurant parking lot in."

"Okay, but if the ersatz waitress is the one who actually fell from the tower, where was Anne? Slim told us he heard the scream when he got to the top and then crossed over to see Anne...the body in the river—there's nowhere to hide on a water tower."

"There's nowhere to hide on the outside, but maybe Anne was on the inside. Slim saw the body in the water and then raced back down to try to grab it from the river before it floated to the dam. If someone was hiding in the tower, she would've had plenty of time to get out and climb down while Slim was chasing after the body."

Weston titled his head up toward the ceiling. "I hear what you're saying...and your theory is plausible, but you shouldn't overthink this. It's been my experience that these things usually have a way of working out for the best."

"Was you getting your toe shot off, your house blown up, and your car impounded...all in addition to being poisoned—twice, what you'd call working out for the best?"

"Those were merely a series of isolated incidents...besides, Slim thinks I should be able to get my car back soon now that the investigation has shifted gears." Weston stood from his chair to join Becky on the couch. "You fret too much. You should learn to relax more...enjoy the moment, such as the rare moments when we have the couch all to ourselves."

Part Four

Chapter 37

Anne snuck up the fire escape to the loft her father had bought for her during her bohemian twenties. She hadn't been back in ages, but she never had the heart to part with it. She flicked on the fluorescent lights hanging from the ceiling. Despite the neighborhood having undergone gentrification over a decade ago, the space retained its industrial feel.

Anne opened her laptop on the counter separating the galley kitchen from the rest of the loft. She logged into the moderator's private meeting room. "Hello."

"Thank you for agreeing to meet with me before our next council session. I thought you should know that many of the members are growing restive."

Anne couldn't help but roll her eyes, momentarily forgetting that her laptop's camera was on.

"I suggest that you start employing a bit more circumspection in your future decisions," said the moderator. "I suspect if the council knew the full details of your activity over the past couple of days, they would characterize your actions as impetuous...not exactly a great attribute for a leader."

"I admit my plan experienced some setbacks due to unanticipated mishaps."

"I'm a bit surprised that you had a plan at all."

Anne frowned. "I don't think I appreciate your tone."

"Then you certainly won't appreciate what I have to say next. You approached this council during a difficult time of transition precipitated by your predecessor exhibiting very poor judgement, nearly exposing our operation. The council was impressed with your decisiveness and willingness to make personal sacrifices—as well as, of course, the considerable resources you stood to inherit from your father's passing. However, since you've resurfaced from your disappearance, I haven't seen any evidence of that hoped for leadership potential. I think I ought to remind you that we aren't a social club. Council leaders don't simply step down; they either succeed or get taken down. The world already assumes that you're dead; there would be little risk to making that assumption a reality."

Anne bit her tongue to keep silent.

The moderator sighed. "Believe it or not, I'm on your side. You bring a lot to the table and have much to offer, but you haven't been playing straight with the council…haven't shown us all your cards. I have it on good authority that you acquired the compound that you last reported to this council was still in development."

"I hadn't yet acquired it at the time of our last meeting, and so I wasn't certain that it was completed."

"I also happen to know, through several of my police contacts, you were implicated in the poisoning of that group of individuals who've run afoul of this council before."

"Yes, but what on the face of it may seem like petty revenge was actually the first human trial of the untested compound. After all, if it had turned out that the product kills those who ingest it, then there wouldn't be anyone left to pay for the cure. I'm pleased to report that all five test subjects survived."

"You were likewise implicated in the attempted poisoning of the town's water supply where some of them reside."

"Since the test subjects effectively became patients zero, I decided to set our plan into motion there. Doesn't it make sense for the next round of cases to occur in the same area soon after?"

The moderator paused before answering. "Yes, I suppose it does, but although you seem to have an answer for everything, it doesn't change the fact that your work was slapdash. If the compound is isolated and the analyte identified, then the plan is over before it's begun."

"I suspect your contacts also informed you that the compound hasn't been discovered, or else you wouldn't bother with this dressing down, but rather you would've proceeded with that more definitive measure you alluded to a moment ago."

"Yes, that's correct. It's been presupposed by those in law enforcement who make such determinations—due in large part to the remains of the body that was discovered, who I can confidently assume wasn't you—that you were unsuccessful in your ill-conceived attempt to poison the town's water supply. Unofficially at least, the authorities deem the question of your disappearance resolved, since they have a credible eyewitness who saw you atop that water tower and then you subsequently falling to what would ultimately become your gruesome demise. Given the many government contracts your father's company is involved with and your standing in the state's literary community as well as a desire not to create widespread panic concerning the generally vulnerable condition of small town water supplies, the powers that be don't intend to go public with their conclusions. Instead, they'll quietly consider the matter closed in order to avoid the embarrassment of admitting to have held in such high esteem someone whom they now presume—thanks in no small part to the shoddiness of your recent efforts—to be a complete crackpot with motives known only to herself, which works out nicely in your favor, though unfortunately undoes your attempt to take out of the equation that group who has shined a light on our operation in the past."

"So where does that leave me with the council?" Anne asked.

"That depends...I haven't yet shared with the council the most recent information I've received from my contacts regarding your escapade at the water tower, and since the authorities intend to keep it out of the press, there's no reason they'd ever have to know about it— that being the case, I believe I could forestall a vote of no confidence."

Anne stared at the screen for a moment. "What's in it for you?"

"A twenty percent stake in your father's...rather, I should say your offshore holding company that you seem to think is such a secret."

Anne shook her head. "Ten percent."

"Fifteen...or this moderator does an immoderate amount of talking at the next council meeting."

"Fine, fifteen percent it is."

"Excellent...that appeases me, but about half the council members still want you out, so they'll also have to be appeased. Do you happen to have any of the product left so that they might have it analyzed in their own private labs?"

"No, I'm afraid it's all gone, but what if I eliminated—once and for all—that band of interlopers who've caused this council so much vexation in the past?"

"Yes," said the moderator, "I believe that would go a long way toward restoring their confidence in you."

Chapter 38

Kate sat apprehensively in the waiting room outside the vice president's office who had putatively been her supervisor. During her time with the company, she'd never actually had occasion to sit on the couch outside her boss's office; he would always come to her. The couch's fabric had a luxurious feel, but the padding underneath offered little give, as if she were sitting on a finely upholstered park bench.

Kate hoped the exit interview would merely be a formality consisting of a few pleasantries, a turning over of the research she'd requested for a couple of her own pet projects, then finally a handshake and a general wish for success in the future. When the executive assistant informed her that she could go in, her hopes for a breezy meeting were quickly dashed. Both the company's vice presidents stood as she entered the office.

Her former boss came around his desk and hugged her awkwardly. "Thank you for coming, Kate." He gestured to an empty chair in front of his desk situated next to the other VP. "It's very good to see you again."

Kate turned to the female vice president as she sat down. "It's good to see you two again too."

Her erstwhile boss retook his seat. "I'll get right to it Kate. As you are well aware, this has not been a banner year for our company. It started off with the death of our founder and is ending with the disappearance of his daughter…a disappearance that from what little the authorities have divulged is becoming more perplexing and problematic by the day—not to mention that unfortunate business you were regrettably on the receiving end of involving our now-disgraced former colleague."

"I'm sorry for your troubles," said Kate, "but it's no longer *our* company…rather, it's yours and not mine."

The female vice president sighed. "That's true Kate, but we've been talking lately…a lot, and in short we'd like to change that."

Kate nodded. "I appreciate the offer, but I don't want my job back—just driving through the front gate had me on pins and needles. The thought of working in my old lab again is…disquieting."

The VP behind the desk shook his head. "No, that's not what we had in mind either. This is embarrassing to admit, but Anne Hedonia hoodwinked us into making her president of this company. At the time it made sense to us; on the public side it offered some continuity to have a family member take over, and on our side—given the recent events that were just coming to light—it would allow us a chance, or so we thought, to get in front of the havoc caused by our company's third vice president…without interference from the president, since she would essentially be a figurehead only."

"Again," added the female vice president, "'or so we thought.'"

"Correct." The male vice president leaned back in his chair. "Now, just as we've managed to mostly put that unfortunate chapter involving the company's rogue senior executive behind us, this new situation emerges with our president…and with the recent past as our teacher, we've learned to expect an extensive and potentially expensive fallout."

"I feel for your predicament," Kate said, "but I still don't see what any of this has to do with me."

"We want you to become our company's new president," replied the female vice president.

"You're well respected in the industry," added the male vice president. "You have an uncheckered history with the company, whereas the rest of us are still operating amidst a miasma of misgivings...and most importantly, you understand the science."

"Do you have any idea how degrading it was taking orders from someone who doesn't know a phlebotomy from a lobotomy?" asked the female vice president. "There's no profession, if you can even call it that, more self-important than a poet...here, read my bumptious nonsense—and if you don't get it, then it just means you're stupid, because I'm smart and that's that. I always knew the empress had no clothes."

The male vice president made a calming gesture. "Okay, I think we're drifting away from the matter at hand. As you can see, Anne rubbed some of us the wrong way from the very beginning; however, now isn't the time to dwell on the past but rather to look toward the future, and we think our future is brighter with you as our president."

"You're pretty much the antithesis of Anne," said the female vice president, "which makes you exactly who we're looking for right now...and if we don't provide a positive update for the end-of-the-year board meeting next week about our search for a new president who can hit the ground running, we'll likely be demoted to the mailroom."

The vice president behind the desk shook his head. "No, we don't really get that much mail these days. They'll just fire us—happy holidays."

"Wow." Kate looked up at the ceiling. "This is a lot to process. I mean, I always thought there was more that we could be doing as a company...inefficiencies that should be corrected, but I'm due to get married soon and then go on my honeymoon."

"Congratulations!" The female vice president's face transitioned in a split-second from delight to distress. "When?"

"On New Year's Day."

"Oh, how wonderful," said the male vice president. "Where is the happy occasion to be held?"

"Well...we haven't exactly worked that out yet."

"I see, and how about the honeymoon?"

"Those details are likewise somewhat up in the air at the moment."

The male vice president placed his elbows on his desk. "Then this is what I propose. You accept our offer and take the job as president. It comes with perks...one of which is that the former president's house down the road is actually owned by the company, as it was built for the purpose of entertaining and lodging visitors and prospective clients. I know, of course, that you've been a guest at the main house, but I don't know if you're familiar with the outbuildings on the estate, the most prominent of which is a charming barn that was converted earlier this year into some sort of an event space as I understand it. Invite your wedding guests to stay over for a New Year's Eve party and then get married there the next day."

The female vice president nodded. "The house will

otherwise be unoccupied, since we'd intended to put up several visiting politicians and dysenteries that'll be attending the fundraiser we're hosting at Navy Pier on New Year's Eve, but with the recent events…well, we weren't sure the house would be available in time, so we booked them all hotel rooms in the city instead."

"Fundraiser?" asked Kate.

The vice president behind the desk smiled. "Yes, it's a gala we've been planning since the beginning of the year, scheduled to fall fast on the heels of what we had anticipated would be something of a victory lap board meeting. We'll be raising money to modernize several of the city's more outdated public libraries—swapping out stacks with computer carrels, getting rid of old books and replacing them with new 5G tablets…that sort of thing. Nothing you need to be concerned about on the weekend of your wedding, but then after your wedding is over, we'll have you start working the following Monday to help put our anxious stakeholders at ease. Work hard for the next six months…then come summertime, take a month off to have your honeymoon on the company's dime—anywhere you want to go. Consider it a signing bonus."

Kate exhaled. "That's an intriguing offer."

Chapter 39

Anne drove her assistant's car down the dirt road to the remote lab. The frozen ground made the potholes all the more punishing on the car's tires and the driver's spine. She swerved to avoid as many as she could but having lived most of her life in the city with a car service at her beck and call, she'd never developed into much of a motorist. Anne figured her assistant's skills as a chauffeur were what she would miss most.

Anne parked in front of the trailer to find the young laboratorian she'd spoken to during her previous visit sitting on the front steps, smoking a cigarette. She rolled down her window. "You know those things are full of noxious chemicals?"

"Yeah, so's my lab, and the ventilation system in there isn't exactly up to OSHA standards." The laboratorian flicked his cigarette away as he approached the car. "Where's your friend?"

"We had something of a falling out, I'm afraid."

"That's too bad—she was cute. So what can I do for you?"

"I need an aerosol version of the product."

The laboratorian tapped his fingers on the roof of the car. "It'll take time…several weeks at least."

"I need it within several days."

"No way—even if I skip Christmas and put all the other projects I'm in the middle of on the back Bunsen burner, which would be exorbitantly expensive…for you, it would be chemically impossible to resynthesize the compound in anything less than a month."

Anne held the canister containing the product out the window. "You don't need to resynthesize it—just turn this solid into a gas and separate it into two containers."

"That's easier said than done."

"I'm not asking if it's easy. I'm asking if you can do it. I'm willing to pay that exorbitant price to back burner your other work."

"The aerosol will be less potent than the crystals—the effects may not last as long."

"That's fine…I intend to have a captive audience in an enclosed space."

"I don't need to hear anything more about that." The laboratorian took the canister. "I can have it ready for you by the end of next week."

"I'll see you next Friday then."

"All right, I'll be here, looking like somebody who hasn't slept in a week and has aged half a decade."

"Don't worry…the haggard look is sexy."

"Well, in case it isn't, I know money always is." The laboratorian grinned. "Payment is due upon receipt."

"You may consider it a belated Christmas gift."

Chapter 40

Becky dragged Weston like a recalcitrant mule to the small waiting area near the dressing rooms. "I need you to hold my purse while I try on these clothes."

"Why do I have to hold your purse? I'm pretty sure they've got hooks back in those dressing rooms."

"The hooks are for hanging the hangers."

"Are you telling me that you can't spare one hook for your purse?"

Becky shook her head. "No, I'm telling you that it was your suggestion to let me pick out the clothes I wanted for my Christmas presents, rather than you buying them and then me returning them. I bet you thought you were being pretty clever, thinking you could just hand over your credit card while you stayed home and watched football all day. Well, guess what, you're not off the hook...you are the hook—for my purse. It's what married men who get out of wrapping gifts for their wives do."

Weston stuck out his index finger, and Becky hung her purse on it. He felt his finger nearly dislocate. "What do you have in here?"

"Just all the stuff I need."

"Apparently not, if you're leaving it with me. It's not too late to leave and do some online shopping instead—think of the selection."

"You can't buy jeans online."

"I'm certain that you can."

"Not if you want them to fit right."

Weston sat down as Becky departed for the dressing rooms. He turned to a man in his late twenties who also uncomfortably held a purse. "Sometimes I miss the pandemic."

The young man nodded. "Yeah, quarantining had its upsides."

"So whose purse are you holding—your mama's?"

"I'm not that young," the man said with a laugh. "It's my fiancée's."

"And she's already got you holding her purse...just a piece of friendly advice, don't let her go believing that she's smarter than you or you'll never get another day off in your life. If she figures out that she's the one with the brains, she'll stop being your spouse and start being your supervisor. Do you think cleaning out the garage or going to pick up dogfood is work for a supervisor or an underling? Let me ask you another question. Do you have a comfortable recliner?"

"Sure," answered the young man.

"Then when your fiancée starts believing that she's smarter than you, you might as well sell it to one of your single buddies, because you won't have time to sit in it anymore...and don't think she won't have some ideas about how to spend the money you get for it either. But here's what you can do to get her off that high horse— when you two leave this store, take her to the movies. Buy her a big soda...then when she inevitably has to go use the restroom in the middle of the film, move seats. She'll come back, looking around for you in the dark down at the front of the theater until you wave at her from the rear. She'll be all embarrassed when she finally spots you, but when she sits down, tell her, 'Hey, it's okay you didn't remember where we were sitting—I'm just lucky to have a gal as beautiful as you.' You see, it's the little things that make a marriage work."

"So how long have you two been married, if you don't mind my asking?"

"Over a year now...most days I barely regret it at all." Weston's cellphone vibrated; he pulled it from his pocket to see who it was. "Hey, Ed...no, I know you're calling from Kate's phone...hmm, that's little more than a week away—if I knew I was going to die in less than a week I'd say yes unequivocally...I'm just joshing you, old friend, I'd be proud to be your best man next weekend...that's a surprising choice of venue, but as long as there's still wine in the cellar, then it's good by me...okay, see you soon." Weston returned his phone to his pocket. "Another poor bastard."

Becky emerged excitedly from the dressing rooms. "Kate called a couple of minutes ago while I was in the middle of changing...she's asked me to be her maid of honor."

"You're married, so you'd be the matron of honor."

"Nope."

Weston tilted his head. "Nope to the matron part or the married part?"

"You ever call me a matron again, and it'll be the latter."

"Wait...you took your phone in with you?"

"Sure, I need it."

Weston held up her purse. "But you told me all the stuff you needed is in here."

"Come on, it looks like now you'll have to buy me a new dress too."

Weston stood reluctantly and gave the young man a knowing look. "Sure, maybe after that we can go see a movie."

Chapter 41

Having HALO jumped into the Pacific, the Pirate Hunter gathered his parachute as he treaded water. He tied a spare diving belt from his front pack around the chute so that it would sink into the ocean. P.H. was confident that his chute had opened under the radar of the jerry-rigged pirate ship patrolling these waters, but he didn't want to leave it floating on the surface to give away his position as he dived down to the wreckage below.

P.H. donned his rebreather apparatus and his scuba fins, then swam in the direction of his sinking parachute. The water felt as cold as his native Lake Michigan in springtime, but the vastness of the Pacific imbued the seawater with a deeper sort of darkness. He looked back up toward the water's surface to the see the beam of a ship's searchlight sweep above him. The pirates wouldn't be able to spot him at this depth, but just the same he'd hoped they were up there because of dumb luck rather than having heard him splash down.

P.H. continued his dive and soon found the wreckage just where it'd been reported. If the pirates above knew that a coast-guard transport helicopter carrying surface-to-surface missiles had crashed in the waters surrounding the port city that they were currently blockading, then the city would likely soon fall under their control. He swam through a breach in the helicopter's cargo hold and used his dive light to find the stack of missiles that had toppled over in the crash. He set to work affixing individual charges to each of the warheads.

If my schedule keeps, thought the Pirate Hunter, *I should soon be done with this Westcoast special detail and back home in time for dinner tomorrow.* When P.H. turned to swim out of the aircraft, he saw something slither from the cockpit. He had never before encountered an eel. He literally felt out of his depth, but P.H. figured that if he didn't mess with it, then it probably wouldn't mess with him. As he swam toward the breach in the hull, something moved around his leg.

He drew his diving knife from the sheath on his thigh and slashed at the eel…wrapped around his ankle. *This is no eel*, P.H. realized, *my problem just got eight times worse.* He espied several more tentacles extending toward him in the murky darkness. He hacked wildly as the suction cups lining the tentacles groped for purchase on his body. Then P.H. felt a tentacle he didn't see twist and tighten around his neck, knocking the rebreather from his mouth.

The tentacles pulled him closer to the cockpit. First he saw two glowing eyes within, then the head of the Giant Pacific Octopus tilted back to reveal its enormous beak. *What I wouldn't give for a speargun.* As the sea monster pulled P.H. nearer its maw, his arms and legs became more entangled in the flailing tentacles. With his knife, he made a final stab toward the head of the octopus, but the tentacle wrapped around his wrist squeezed harder, and the blade fell from his hand.

P.H. wrestled his left hand free up to his forearm, affording him enough range of motion to reach the detonation button clipped to his belt to set off the explosives. He flicked open the safety cover. The giant octopus tilted its head down, revealing its eyes once more. P.H. felt the grip of the tentacles loosen slightly, as if the tiny brains in each of the arms were distracted by a pressing conversation with the larger centralized brain.

Suddenly the octopus vanished in a turbid cloud, turning the dark waters completely opaque, despite the dive light dangling from the Pirate Hunter's belt. P.H. swam through the broken windshield of the cockpit, racing to get clear of the cephalopod ink and reattach his rebreather.

****

H.P. woke up, gasping for air. As he caught his breath, he stared up at the dark tentacles undulating across his bedroom ceiling, the moonlight casting shadows from the tree branches outside his window. H.P. turned to glance at his alarm clock, then he took his mobile phone off the nightstand and noticed a new email from Edwin with the subject line: Groomsman?

Chapter 42

Slim sat in his patrol car, watching the last-minute shoppers hurrying into and out of the strip-mall parking lot. The roads were covered in a light patina of snow—not enough to call in the snowplows, but a sufficient amount to make patches of ice difficult for motorists to see, especially those more focused on their shopping lists than their driving. Slim had already issued nine warnings that morning for driving too fast for conditions, though not a single ticket, but still no one had offered a merry Christmas or even a nod of gratitude for not costing them extra money during the holidays…just harrumphs for having been delayed all of five minutes to be reminded to slow down when the roads are slick.

Slim's cellphone buzzed on the passenger's seat. "Jell-O…yeah, I can work your shift tomorrow…I know it's Christmas Eve, but my boy is at his mom's all weekend, so I'm free…no problem."

An SUV coming out of the parking lot made a left turn against the light into the far lane. Slim hit his red and blues, pulling off the frontage road where he'd been parked in plain sight. He quickly caught up to the SUV, and the driver pulled over. As Slim ran the license plate, the driver rolled down his window, stuck his arm out, and beckoned in the direction of the squad car. *This had better be good*, Slim thought as he exited his vehicle.

As Slim approached, the middle-aged driver leaned

out his window. "I know I ran that red light back there, but I'm in a hurry, and I don't need no song and dance about the rules of the road—just write me a ticket, if that's what you're gonna do, so I can be on my way."

"10-4." Slim returned to his patrol car, opened his citation book, and very painstakingly wrote up a ticket for a red-light violation, improper lane usage, and a windshield obstruction for the air freshener hanging from the rearview mirror. His phone rang again. "Yellow...no, I can talk...unexpected family in town, huh...sure, I can cover your shift...I know it's Christmas Day, but my boy will be with his mom...you bet."

Slim exited his vehicle and reapproached the SUV. The grumpy man rolled down his window again. "Took you long enough."

"I got a cramp in my hand from all the writing I did." Slim held up the tickets. "I got you for—"

The man snatched the tickets out of Slim's hand. "I can read. Are we done here?"

Slim sighed. "Somebody's bound to get hurt if you keep driving like an idget."

"Happy freakin' holidays," said the man as he rolled up his window. Slim stood along the side of the road as the driver sped off. He considered running back to his squad car to give chase and issue the driver another citation for speeding...or maybe pulling his sidearm from its holster and shooting out the SUV's tires, but instead he walked slowly back to his cruiser. His cellphone began to ring as he opened the driver's side door.

"Hello."

"Slim, it's Edwin. I hope I'm not phoning you at a bad time."

"It ain't a bad time in the sense that I can't talk."

"I'm not sure what you mean, but I'm calling to ask if you're available to be a groomsman in my wedding next weekend."

"I'd be honored, Ed."

"You sure you can make it, given that it's a holiday weekend?"

"I know it's New Year's next weekend, but a couple of officers in my department owe me a favor, so I'm certain that I can get the time off."

"Splendid—merry Christmas, young man…if you go in for that sort of thing."

Chapter 43

Weston and Becky sipped hot cocoa on the couch, while Van played with Ance in the mound of torn wrapping paper in front of the Christmas tree. Lance shook his final present. "What's in this one? I already got all the robots I asked for."

"Open it and find out," said Becky.

Lance unwrapped the gift with alacrity and threw off the top of the apparel box to reveal a cardigan sweater. "What is it?"

"What do you mean 'what is it?' " asked Becky. "It's a sweater to keep you warm."

Lance lifted the sweater out of the box as if pulling a dead squirrel from a clogged downspout. "It has buttons."

"They put me in mind of a varsity sweater," Becky replied. "I don't know...I thought it looked a little more sophisticated than your hoodies."

"But I like my hoodies."

"I wear hoodies," added Vance. "So does most everybody on campus."

Weston yawned. "Me too. The hoods are great for taking naps."

"I know you guys like your hoodies, but I just thought Lance might also like something that made him look a bit more mature. Try it on."

Lance begrudgingly donned the sweater. "I don't

feel more mature. I feel hot." He ran a finger over the buttons skeptically.

"You might as well have gotten him a smoking jacket," said Weston.

Becky sighed. "Fine, I'll exchange it for yet another sweatshirt."

"I still like the robots," said Lance.

"Vancy, what was your favorite gift?" Becky asked.

"Getting my report card yesterday and learning that I didn't flunk out of college."

"I wouldn't exactly call academic probation a Christmas miracle," Weston said, "but I'm glad we can continue with our plans to convert your bedroom into my study."

Becky smacked Weston's shoulder. "No one's taking over your room…until you graduate—and then we'll talk about making it into an arts and craft room."

Weston grinned. "But Becca, we already have two rooms for farts and crap—one upstairs and the other down."

"I get it—you mean our bathrooms." Lance offered an air high-five. "Good one."

Becky stood from the couch. "On that lovely note, let's have some breakfast."

****

Weston pulled back the hood of his sweatshirt from over his eyes when the doorbell rang. As he got off the couch to answer the door, Lance looked up from the living room carpet where he was playing with his robots. "When's dinner?"

"We didn't eat breakfast until after we opened presents, which pushed our lunch back to two, so I imagine dinner will be an hour or so after your bedtime.

Are you hungry already?"

"No, I guess I'm just a little bored with these robots. I think I'll go upstairs to see what Van's doing."

"Okay, just don't wake your mom and Ance from their nap when he kicks you out of his room." Weston opened the front door as Lance climbed the staircase. "Merry Christmas, Hamish."

H.P. stepped inside. "It'd be merrier still if you didn't call me that anymore."

"Relax, no one heard. I never understood why you didn't like that name. It's not nearly as odious as your surname."

H.P. handed Weston a bottle of wine. "Feel free to remove the cork and use it to plug your mouth."

"Depriving all and sundry of my greatest gift on Christmas day?"

H.P. looked about the living room. "Where are the sundries, by the by?"

"Upstairs—the girls are taking a nap and the boys are probably rotting their brains in front of some screen or other." Weston picked up the TV remote and turned off the football game he'd lost interest in an hour ago.

"You sure it's all right that I'm over here? After all, Christmas is a time for families."

"Christmas morning is a time for families; Christmas evening is a time for friends and family. Besides, Kate is over near campus visiting a former colleague who'll be a bridesmaid, and Ed's in town getting the last of his things out of storage, so they're stopping by later to talk with Becca—and I guess me—about wedding arrangements…when it comes to those sorts of conversations, I say the more the merrier."

"I think what you mean is misery loves company."

H.P. followed Weston into the kitchen. "I was surprised when Ed told me that Kate had asked Becky to be her matron of honor."

"I don't think Kate has many close friends. The way I understand it, her colleague on campus is more of a work friend, and the other bridesmaid is that roommate from college she mentioned whom she hasn't seen since the beginning of the year." Weston set the bottle on the counter. "She and Ed are similar in that respect. He asked Slim to be his other groomsman, and I don't believe he even knows his real name."

"Well, he doesn't know mine either, and I'll thank you to keep it that way."

"Speaking of people being irrationally sensitive about what they're called, Becca prefers maid of honor to matron."

"Really? Whenever I think of a maid of honor, I always picture a woman standing next to the bride in a scanty French maid's uniform."

"And I'll thank you not to do that at this wedding." Weston handed H.P. a corkscrew and then took two wineglasses down from the cupboard.

"Oh, I brought this bottle for dinner."

"Ed's bringing over a jug from his cache of wine in storage."

"Is he still convinced that every wine improves with age?"

"Even if it's aged on the concrete floor of a non-climate-controlled storage unit, which is why I want to drink this bottle now before everyone else gets here?"

"Ah, I see your point." H.P. set to uncorking the bottle.

"Slim's supposed to stop by after his shift with a

batch of his infamous venison stew."

"If I had to choose a wine to pair with deer meat, it would likely come in a jug."

"I think Becca's sister is coming over later too with her *siete*-layer dip."

"Nothing says yuletide like tortilla chips."

"I wouldn't be surprised if Kim spelled out Feliz Navidad in red and green salsas, but you won't hear me complain about hosting Christmas dinner. I don't have to drive anywhere…everyone brings the food and drink to me."

H.P. poured the wine. "That's the holiday spirit."

"I'll drink to that…and just about anything else you've got. While we're on the subject of ships in bottles and gifts that keep on giving—"

"Did I miss a page of the script?" interrupted H.P. "I don't recall talking about either of those things."

Weston sniffed the wine in his glass. "You mentioned holiday spirits. I thought you meant giving liquor as a gift…you give it once, then you drink it with the recipient, and it gives again—like having your cake and eating it too."

"I don't think so. First of all, wines aren't classified as spirits. Second of all, you can't have your cake and also eat it—that's precisely the meaning of the apothegm. And third of all, I think the premise of your analogy is a bit of a stretch…but what about that ship in a bottle business?"

"Nothing exemplifies Christmastime quite so much as critiquing a friend's figure of speech. Someone should've shoved a red pen down your stocking, or perhaps up someplace else…but I digress. So, like a ship inside a bottle, the contents within a wine bottle can—

figuratively, mind you—act as a transport of sorts if drunk in sufficient quantities."

"First of all, that's not an overstretched analogy but rather a full-on hyperextension."

"Given the season," Weston said, "would it be possible to find it in your Scrooge-like heart to skip an 'of all' or two?"

"And lastly, but not leastly—I submit that you drink too much."

"Isn't this a fun time for an intervention?" Weston sipped his wine.

"Weren't you clumsily attempting to broach a subject before we set off on this tangent?"

"Yes, I was about to suggest once more—given how well we get along—that we collaborate on another book...my Spinster, but maybe a new character from you, or the Pirate Hunter again if you like. I'm sure one's as good as another—nearly interchangeable I imagine."

H.P. brought his wineglass to his nose. "I have yet to hear from the university about whether they want me to resume my teaching duties next semester, so I may well have some extra time on my hands."

"Great...about you being amenable to another collaboration—not about you being fired. Anyway, I had some thoughts about structure. I say we eschew our conventional five-act format in favor of a two-act narrative...three at the most."

"I concur. A five-acter seems a little staid these days...maybe even antiquated."

"I couldn't agree more—that fourth act ends up feeling so on and on, as if the reader can't help but think: I know...you're setting up the denouement—just get to it already."

H.P. took a sip of wine. "Right, those extraneous acts lend themselves to too much exposition—this happens and then that happens."

"I don't think exposition is our problem, but rather that our chatty characters like to have a conversation about every little thing that happens to them."

"I disagree with your characterization of our characters—or at least mine, but let's place that particular facet of this literary discussion in abeyance for now. I have a new idea that I've been mulling over for a while."

"I'm intrigued—what is it?" asked Weston.

"How about we include some seemingly incongruous dream sequences that actually foreshadow the coming narrative?"

"My hearing must be going. I could've sworn you told me that you had a 'new idea' you were mulling over."

H.P. frowned. "It's new to me."

"And no one else…it's such a hackneyed gimmick—'Oh, look how clever I'm being by predicting what happens next.' Of course you can predict what happens next, you're the one who thought it all up. Interspersing portentous dream episodes that only vaguely relate to the story is the oldest new idea I've ever heard of."

"I hope you intend to end fewer of your sentences with prepositions in our collaboration than you do in our conversation."

"The oldest new idea I've ever heard of—jackass."

H.P. nodded. "Yep, this project is off to about as auspicious a start as our last."

****

Lance answered the front door. Slim entered with a large pot. "Merry Christmas, buddy."

"You too…what's in there?"

"Venison stew—it's been simmering all day. My boy can't get enough of it. Are you going to try some?"

"Dear meat, no thanks—signed me."

Becky crossed the living room and kissed Slim on the cheek. "Here, I can take that. I've got a trivet set up on the dining room table for it. You can see it's a full house, but you know everybody, so grab a beer from the fridge and make yourself at home."

Slim entered the kitchen to find Edwin noshing on seven-layer dip and Weston chopping fruit at the counter as H.P. stirred up a cocktail in a pitcher using red wine from a jug.

"Season's greetings, young man." Edwin wiped his right hand on his shirt and then shook hands with Slim. "All my groomsmen in the same room—how nice."

"We don't have any wassail, but care for a glass of sangria?" asked H.P.

"I don't know what either of those things are, so I think I'll just have a beer."

"Kim brought over some bottles of Mexican beer to go with her dip," said Weston.

Slim gave his friend a look.

Weston grinned. "But there's also some domestic beer in the back of the refrigerator that might be more to your liking."

Slim procured a can of beer and popped the top. "Ed, do I need to rent a tuxedo for this shindig next weekend?"

"I'm afraid so," Edwin answered. "I tried to talk Kate into letting us wear those tux T-shirts that I've always found so amusing, but she was having none of it."

Weston started slicing a lime. "Smart lady."

H.P. began pouring sangria into glasses. "So the plan is that we drive up on New Year's Eve—get things ready during the day, have a little party that night, and then the ceremony will commence at noon the following day?"

Edwin nodded. "That's correct. Kate's other bridesmaids won't be able to arrive until New Year's Day due to previously planned NYE engagements. It'll be a small affair—not including the wedding party, we're anticipating a couple dozen guests. There'll also be some staff on hand to cater the lunch afterward…oh, and the ceremony won't actually begin until 12:30— apparently starting weddings on the half-hour is a tradition."

"It's considered good luck if the ceremony occurs while the minute hand is moving up the clock face rather than down," said Weston. "I learned that myself about this same time last year."

"That's interesting," Edwin replied. "Do you also happen to know why they're called clock hands instead of arms? I've always wondered since they're shaped more like arms than hands."

Weston garnished a glass of sangria with a slice of lime and handed it to Edwin. "Old friend, one thing I'm sure of is that you and Kate will always have plenty to talk about."

Kim entered from the dining room. "Talk about what? It's all dresses and flowers in there. What are you boys chatting about in here?"

"Clocks," answered Weston.

"Fine, don't tell me." Kim took a beer from the

refrigerator. "But I'll need another one of these if I'm expected to listen to any more talk about a wedding that I won't be attending."

"You're invited, of course," said Edwin.

"Thanks, but your fiancée wants a grownup wedding—what bride doesn't—so since my sister is the maid of honor, that means I'll have to take care of Ance."

"We appreciate you staying here while we'll be gone," Weston said.

"Oh, I don't mind really…it's not like I had New Year's plans." Kim pried the cap from her beer with a bottle opener. "Maybe after I put Lance and Ance to bed, I'll have too many of these and drunk dial one of my ex-boyfriends."

Weston shook his head. "I wasn't aware inmates could receive phone calls after hours in prison." Before Kim could rejoin, the doorbell rang. Weston headed toward the living room. "Who could that be…everyone we know is here."

Weston opened the door to find a delivery driver standing on the front porch. "I have a package for Mr. and Mrs. Hubert."

"This isn't their house, but they happen to be here now. You must be Santa Claus to make deliveries on Christmas."

The driver handed over the tall box he held. "No, Santa's the one who paid me three hundred bucks to deliver that package to this address."

"I hope you don't have too many more stops tonight."

"I'm going home." The driver turned back toward his cargo van. "This was my only delivery for the day."

Weston took the box into the dining room and set it

on the table in front of Kate and Becky as the others entered from the kitchen.

"Who's it from?" asked Becky.

"There's no return address," answered Weston, "but it's for Ed and Kate."

Kate unwrapped the package's brown paper to reveal a Styrofoam carton within. She opened the small envelope fastened to the carton and read the typed card aloud. "I look forward to toasting your nuptials." She lifted off the carton top. "It's warm." A clay pot rested in the base of the carton. Kate unwound the cotton batting covering the potted plant to reveal a black orchid.

"It's beautiful," Edwin remarked.

Kate nodded. "And as rare as it is inappropriate."

Part Five

Chapter 44

Weston climbed into the cab of Slim's pickup idling in the rent-a-car parking lot. "I'm glad to be rid of that rental. The whole time I had it, I never figured out half of the doohickeys that apparently cars come standard with these days. Anyway, thanks for agreeing to drive me over to the impound lot to pick up my old car."

"No sweat." Slim pulled out of the lot. "And I hear you about getting attached to a vehicle. I bought this here truck when I first joined the force. I'll never understand people who're in an all-fire hurry to trade in their cars every couple of years. If you're so anxious to get rid of it, why'd you buy it in the first place?"

"I completely agree with you, which makes me nervous. We sound like a couple of old guys getting ready to reminisce about the days when things were made by hand with pride. The difference between us though is that I actually am old…or at least middle-aged, but you're not even forty yet, so what's your excuse?"

"Us country boys tend to be old-fashioned even before we get over the hill."

Weston watched as the road's white lane markers disappeared under Slim's pickup. Though the snow had melted, the asphalt's surface was still crusted in salt, making the markers difficult to see. "Shouldn't those white lines be like any other color?"

"They can't be no dark color, because then you couldn't see 'em at night."

"They're the lightest possible color, and I can barely see them now."

"You can't make 'em yellow, because that means something different."

"How about fluorescent orange?"

Slim shook his head. "Orange is pretty close to yellow."

"What about bright pink then?"

"Yep, I guess you could make 'em that. Now let me ask you a question: what's really eating you?"

"So you saw Anne on top of that water tower as you were climbing up."

"Affirmative."

"Then before you got to the top, you saw her fall from the other side."

Slim nodded. "Correct."

"But what if it wasn't her body that fell?"

"You mean like if somebody else had been up there with Ms. Hedonia that I hadn't seen from below, and her partner started climbing down just as I was about to the top, but then maybe our bad gal loosened the knot so that her accomplice fell while she hid herself inside the tower and made her escape as I chased after whosoever body that was in the river…yeah, the thought had occurred to me."

"Then might going back to the scene of the original crime be a setup…again?"

"That'd occurred to me too," answered Slim. "But the way I figure it, a criminal as slick and ornery as this Ms. Hedonia could get at anybody almost anywhere if she had a mind to, so why not let her think we're not expecting her if she decides to strike again. Besides, it's Ed and Kate's wedding…living in fear ain't no kind of way to start a life together."

Chapter 45

Kate exited the parking lot of the bridal shop with Becky in the passenger's seat and a white gown laid across the backseat. "Thanks for coming with me to pick out my dress. Since I had to buy off-the-rack due to the compressed nature of our wedding planning, it was nice to have a second opinion from someone who wasn't working on commission."

"Oh, it was fun. For my first wedding, the only criteria I had for my dress was that it be inexpensive and capable of fitting over my very pregnant belly."

"I'm sure you looked radiant."

"I don't know about that, but we had a good time. The reception was like a redo of prom but with booze…that I couldn't drink."

"Well, you'll have a wine cellar at your disposal for this reception."

Becky sighed. "That sounds nice, but something tells me that I should keep my wits about me this weekend."

"You think Anne's still alive, don't you?"

"I wouldn't be surprised if she were."

"And that she sent those ominous flowers on Christmas."

"The thought had crossed my mind."

"Mine too…about eight dozen times."

"And you still feel comfortable getting married up

there…in the same space where she made that comment about hothouse flowers earlier this month?"

Kate shook her head. "Comfortable…I wouldn't say that, but I figure someone as cunning as she's proven herself to be could cause trouble for us just about anywhere, so why not let her think she has the home field advantage to make her move? I have a marriage and a new job to look forward to next year. I don't want to begin either by being afraid, so let her do her worst. I'll be ready for the fiend."

"Okay—you've convinced me. Maybe I will have some wine then."

"Just keep the bottle handy in case you need to bash it over a certain party crasher's head."

"Does Ed know what a firecracker he's getting hitched to?"

Kate smiled. "My Eddie has no idea."

"You're really head over heels for that guy, aren't you?"

"I've been trying to land that big fish for years, and now I can hardly believe that I'm actually going to reel him in tomorrow. I know to some he may seem more like a whale shark than a marlin, but that brilliant dummy sees the world…the whole universe really, like no one else I've ever met."

"He's certainly unusual." Becky sat up a bit straighter. "I meant to say unique…you know, singular."

"Not for long."

Chapter 46

Edwin examined the untied bowtie around his neck in the mirror of the passenger's side visor. "I think whoever invented ties must've been a sadist."

H.P. pulled onto the interstate's entrance ramp. "Why, because it restricts one of the most vulnerable parts of the body through which we take in all the things we need to live—air, water, nourishment?"

"Yes, that'd be why."

"I was being sarcastic. Anyway, it seems like ties are falling by the wayside these days like hats did in the sixties."

"So you think it'll take a decade for them to fall by the wayside completely? That won't do me much good tomorrow."

H.P. zippered into interstate traffic. "No, I suppose it won't. Besides, I imagine it'll take a bit longer for ties to disappear since they have more of a sartorial stranglehold than hats ever enjoyed."

"So how long do you figure then?"

"I'm no expert on this sort of thing, but I'd say a generation or so."

"What's that…like fifteen years?"

"Maybe thirty, depending on who you ask."

"So my tieless neck should be quite comfortable lying in my coffin."

H.P. shook his head. "It sounds like you're pretty

excited for the big day."

"Is that more sarcasm?"

"Nice…you're getting better at identifying it."

"I'm looking forward to having Kate permanently in my life. I've been alone a long time, though three hundred days out of the year I didn't mind it at all, say sixty or so days my aloneness would border on lonesomeness, and then maybe five days a year I'd get downright lonely."

H.P. nodded. "It's depressing to sleep by yourself on your birthday."

"That reminds me, happy belated birthday."

"Thanks, but let's get back to you and your day tomorrow…so now you won't be lonely anymore."

"Right, that part will be nice, but the other parts that come with it—namely this silly ceremony, monogrammed gifts, and things like…" Edwin took three other ties from the shopping bag on his lap. "…going to a haberdashery to purchase ties for my groomsmen and the salesclerk telling me that it's customary for the groom's tie to be different from the others. Why, out of concern that my bride won't be able to tell us apart? I submit if there was any threat of that, then the couple about to be wed are not a suitable match."

H.P. chuckled. "From what I understand, there's a long tradition of grooms-to-be lamenting the sacrifice of personal freedoms required for domestic bliss, but take heart…when it comes to you, Kate is about the most tolerant woman I've ever met. As for the monogramming, feel free to return the towels I got for you two."

"Are you being sarcastic again?"

"I wish."

"I think my case of cold feet mostly has to do with the thought of standing in front of people tomorrow, repeating the minister's words, and wearing clothes that aren't my own."

"Your cold feet might also have to do with my heater not working very well." H.P. adjusted a knob on the dashboard.

"Some music might settle my nerves. Do you mind if we listen to one of my theremin CDs?"

"I don't mind, but the CD player is busted."

"Aren't you about due for a new car?" asked Edwin.

"I was planning to get one in the spring, but if it ends up that I'm out of a job, then I won't really have any place to drive."

"You're always welcome to drive up to visit me and Kate on the weekends, or better yet I can bring my telescope down and stay with you during the week, since it sounds like Kate will be rather busy with her new job for the next few months. It'd be like old times."

H.P. poked at the buttons on the radio in search of music. "Why don't we see what the new year brings before we start making plans to relive old times?"

Chapter 47

Weston pretended to be asleep in the driver's seat of his sedan as Slim parked his truck behind him in the circular driveway of the ranch house. Slim got out of his pickup and knocked on the car's trunk as he approached the driver's side door.

Weston opened his eyes. "Oh, hey, Slimpoke...I was just resting my eyes a bit while I waited for you."

"What you need to do is stop resting your foot on that accelerator, or instead of being rested you're liable to be arrested."

"Wordplay isn't your forte, my friend." Weston exited his car.

"I take it we beat the others here."

"Yeah, I went inside, but there's some workers in the kitchen prepping for the banquet tomorrow, and then a cleaning crew spread out through the rest of the house. It seems the cops left behind quite a mess, and I was informed that the staff wasn't allowed back in until earlier today. I decided to wait out here so that I wouldn't be in the way."

"That's uncharacteristically considerate of you."

"Not really...I was afraid that if I loitered for too long someone might put me to work. Let's go have a look in the barn."

The two walked the short path to the barn and opened the side door to the sound of sawing. An old man in a hoary cowboy hat looked up from a makeshift workbench set up on a pair of sawhorses at the back of the studio. "Oh, don't mind me. I'm just hanging an ax."

"What's it guilty of," asked Weston, "cattle rustling?"

The old man tilted his head sideways.

"Don't mind my friend," said Slim. "He's got a condition…his butt is connected directly to his brain, so you never know what's going to come out of his mouth."

The old man smiled. "I've got a son like that—real smart aleck…never outgrew it neither. Now he teaches grammar to teenagers—serves him right."

"So how'd you bust your ax handle?" asked Slim.

"Some tree limbs came down during the last snowstorm. I cut 'em up with a chainsaw, then started splitting the thicker logs for firewood, but I guess this old piece of hickory didn't care too much for chopping out in the cold."

Weston watched as the old man drew the teeth of a handsaw across the woodgrain of the new handle protruding from the top of a superannuated ax head. "Isn't that a job for the groundskeeper?"

"He's out of town visiting family. I fill in for him from time to time. I was one of them who raised this here barn way back when—you won't find a sturdier barn for miles…though the inside sure has changed in the last year."

Weston picked up the broken ax handle off the floor. "This barn doesn't seem very conducive to manual labor anymore."

The old man shook his head. "No, I guess not, but then there ain't no place else to work out of the cold, so I thought I'd set up in here. Some of the old tools are still stored in the utility closet back there. If I had more time, I'd have sanded the floors to get rid of the blood stain, but I suppose that white tarp I put down will have to do."

Weston looked over at the tarp spread across the floor under several rows of folding chairs. "I'm sure it'll suffice…no one's expecting perfection on such short notice."

Slim nodded. "That's right, old timer, you're the one hanging the ax…there ain't one hanging over you. Is there anything we can do to help you get this place set up for tomorrow?"

"Nah, this barn practically runs itself now. The HVAC and security systems are automated—the only thing for me to do in here was set up them chairs…though I suppose I could use a hand chopping up the last of the logs and then toting them over to the firewood rack."

****

Weston walked with the ax back to the barn as Kate and Becky pulled up and parked behind Slim's truck. Weston waited as the two exited the car.

"Have they got you doing manual labor?" asked Kate.

"It's good for the constitution to work with your hands now and then." Weston kissed his wife.

"We the people doesn't appear to have broken a sweat," said Becky.

"It's cold out here…besides, I prefer to work smarter, not harder."

Kate grinned. "The only work you look like you're doing is walking around with an ax."

"As I say—smarter. I'm returning this to the barn while Slim and some geezer stack a bunch of firewood up by the house. If I time it right, I'll get back just as they're finishing."

The three turned when they heard another vehicle come up the driveway. H.P. and Edwin parked behind Kate's car. The two got out, and the groom-to-be pointed at his best man. "What are you doing with that old ax?"

"How dare you speak to my wife that way," said Weston.

Edwin shook his head. "No, I didn't say old battle ax…that is I didn't mean—"

"He's just tooling with you," interrupted H.P.

Edwin nodded. "Ah, like an ax is a tool."

Kate rolled her eyes. "All right, boys, I could stand here and listen to this all day…well, not all day really, but for a few more minutes at least; however, I should go inside to check on preparations for tomorrow. I'm sure the staff is anxious to finish up and get on with their own New Year's Eve plans."

"We've got loads of stuff in the trunk," added Becky, "so come help me bring it inside."

Weston pointed to Edwin and H.P. as he walked toward the barn. "You heard the lady…get to unloading."

Becky glared at Weston. "You too—go put that thing away and come help."

"But I should check on Slim first."

"I'm sure he can manage—now snap to it."

"That's not a very maidenly way to address the best man." Weston continued to grumble as he entered the barn. "You'd better believe that sort of behavior is going in my report."

Chapter 48

Kate stood statue still in the doorway at the top of the staircase leading down to the wine cellar when Becky happened by. "Is everything okay?"

Kate turned from the darkness below. "I came to pick out some wines for tomorrow…about ten minutes ago. An image popped into my head of Anne hiding down there that night during the blackout while we all looked for her. I'm sure she heard us yelling her name over and over throughout this cavernous house. She must've known how worried we were about her as we searched for her in the dark. How could someone be so cold-blooded to remain hidden like that?"

"You know, you don't have to do this…any of this. Everyone would understand if you wanted to postpone your wedding until another venue could be arranged."

"I wouldn't understand. This house doesn't belong to me or Anne. It belongs to the company that her father built—a man I respected. Now I've been asked to lead his company. What kind of leader would I be if I was frightened out of the home that meant so much to him? Maybe it doesn't make any actual sense, but I feel like getting married here is a chance to erase the negativity Anne left behind."

Becky hugged Kate. "It makes perfect sense…and I have an idea."

****

Becky and Kate stood with flashlights at the top of the cellar stairs as Weston, Edwin, Slim, and H.P. bustled about down in the cellar. Slim blew the dust off a bottle of wine and held it up. "What about this one…it has the sloping shoulders you described?"

Kate shined the beam of her flashlight on the bottle from above. "It looks like a pinot noir…I want chardonnays."

"What's the difference?" Slim asked.

"Pinots are red and chardonnays white," answered H.P.

Slim returned the bottle to the rack. "I haven't seen any white wines yet—only reds and clears."

Weston sighed. "The clear ones are the white wines."

"Somebody might've mentioned that earlier," said Slim.

"If you see any reds you like, feel free to bring them up too," Kate called down. "We can open them tonight for dinner or have them tomorrow. I just wanted to get the whites in the refrigerator, so they'll be cold for the banquet."

Edwin examined a bottle on the rack. "I still say nothing beats a nice jug of wine—they're inexpensive, they consistently taste the same, and they're always enough."

"Since the reception will also be in the barn," said Becky, "we could stock that beverage fridge out there with the white wines."

Kate nodded. "Oh, that's a good idea."

"Do you think that fridge would also have some room for beer?" asked Slim. "I've got a case out in my truck."

Chapter 49

Becky and Kate admired the neatly stacked rows of white wines in the beverage refrigerator as Edwin loaded up a plastic bin with the sports drinks and water bottles that he'd removed. "Should I take these into the main house and put them in one of the kitchen fridges?"

Kate placed her purse atop the short refrigerator. "No, they're both pretty full already. You can just tuck the bin out of sight in the back."

"But they'll get warm," Edwin replied. "What if someone wants a cold bottle of water tomorrow?"

"We'll set the bin outside in the morning to let them get cold again. Then we can backfill the fridge here as the wine is removed."

Edwin smiled. "That's an elegant solution, my dear."

"Why thank you, Eddie." Kate turned her attention to Weston, Slim, and H.P. inspecting the large video screen at the front of the studio. "There's a trick to turning it on."

"What's that?" asked H.P. "Finding the remote?"

"No, it's voice activated," said Becky. "Room, video screen on."

The screen remained unchanged. Kate cleared her throat. "Room, video screen on." Still the screen stayed dormant. "Huh, perhaps it's offline—that's disappointing…I was hoping to tune in some picturesque scenery tomorrow."

Becky smiled. "The scenery last time we were in here was rather picturesque."

"What, did that yogi fellow have mountaintops and rainbows in the background?" asked Weston.

"I don't recall any sort of background," answered Kate.

"The foreground is what really caught the eye," added Becky.

"Some septuagenarian wearing a dashiki and love beads?" Weston asked.

"No, I don't think Panta was in his seventies," said Kate.

Becky nodded. "About half that age, I'd say...though it's difficult to tell someone's age when they're that fit."

Kate rubbed her chin. "And I don't remember him wearing a dashiki."

"All I remember Panta wearing were those little form fitting shorts," said Becky, "so that he could bend over without restriction."

Weston frowned. "Wait, this popinjay was shirtless?"

"Of course," Kate answered, "in order to better demonstrate the poses and show us which muscles to stretch."

Becky raised an eyebrow. "Besides, it'd be a crime to cover up a chiseled torso like his."

"That sounds like an absolutely shameful display." Weston put his hands on his hips. "Ed, what do you make of all this...your fiancée ogling some limber Lothario."

"I don't care what she watches on TV, so long as she doesn't expect me to start doing sit ups and side bends."

Weston shook his head. "Shameful all around—what's become of decency…of morality."

Becky turned to Slim. "While my husband continues to pontificate about moral decay, you're welcome to get the beer from your truck. We saved the bottom shelf for it."

"Much obliged." Slim crossed toward the studio's side door. "And I don't think there's no shame in appreciating the human body. In fact, if you gals have a mind to ogle me as I exit this here barn—you got my permission to go right on ahead and do so."

Weston threw up his arms.

Chapter 50

Slim's cellphone buzzed as he pulled a case of beer from his truck box. He set the beer in the bed of his pickup and took his phone from his pocket. "Yep, this is he...I see...okay, I appreciate you letting me know...10-4." Slim then called one of his contacts. "Hey, get someplace you can talk in private for a minute."

Weston moved toward the back of the barn away from the others. "What's up?"

"I'm calling because I didn't want to unduly alarm the others. I notified the local P.D. that this weekend y'all was planning a return to the scene of the crime as it were and relayed my suspicions that Ms. Hedonia might still be in play, so they agreed to keep an eye on the grounds for suspicious activity. They've been monitoring us down at the station via the security cameras ever since we got here, but I just got a call that they've been locked out of the system. Now it could just be some sort of glitch with the interface between the security network and the proxy server, but then again it might not be. Either way, I'd feel a whole lot better if we vamoosed until everything gets sorted out at the station and them cameras come back online."

"You make me nervous when you start using words like 'interface' and 'proxy.' "

"Look, this may all be nothing...but if it ain't nothing, then it's something—know what I mean?"

"I do indeed," said Weston. "Okay, I'll go suggest we all drive into town for an early dinner."

"That sounds like a good plan. I'll keep watch out here to make sure nobody else is around. With all the workers gone for the day, there shouldn't be anybody but us on the premises."

"All right, we'll be out in a minute." Weston pocketed his phone and rejoined the others in the middle of the large, open room. "Ed, are you starting to get hungry?"

Ed reflexively placed his hand on his belly. "Sure, I could eat."

"Since we'll be here all day tomorrow, why don't we go out for dinner tonight?" Weston asked.

Becky shook her head. "On New Year's Eve without reservations…going out will likely end up being us eating drive-thru in a parking lot."

Weston nodded. "A cheeseburger before all the fancy food we're in store for tomorrow sounds good to me too."

"If you're in the mood for cheese, I thought we could have fondue tonight," said Kate. "It's not fancy, but it might be fun."

"I can't recall the last time I had fondue," H.P. replied, "that does sound fun."

Edwin smiled. "I trust you had the staff prepare a chocolate fondue for our dessert."

"But of course, Eddie," Kate replied. "Sweets for my sweetie."

Weston crossed his arms. "I didn't want to do this, but I'm afraid I'll have to invoke my privilege as best man and demand that we have the rehearsal dinner— which this technically would be—at a restaurant of my choosing."

Edwin frowned. "I'm not familiar with that particular custom."

"No one is," said H.P.

Something caught Kate's attention at the front of the studio. "Hey look, the video screen came on."

The others turned to see an enormous pair of eyes appear as the immense screen brightened. "Hello, good guys."

****

With the binoculars from his glove compartment, Slim scanned the wooded areas beyond the pastures behind the house—no movement anywhere, though it was nearly dark, so if there were assailants lurking among the trees, he figured they'd likely delay making their move until nighttime. He looked to the horizon. The day's last vestiges of oranges and reds were giving way to the encroaching blues and purples.

Slim checked his watch as he returned to his truck. Empty cars sat in the driveway, and the lights were still on in the barn. *Shouldn't they be out here by now arguing about where to go eat?* he thought. Slim looked again at the converted barn; the light through the lone window near the peak of the roof seemed to shine brighter than when he'd left to take a lap around the house, but he attributed the increased brightness to the darker sky above the roofline.

Slim returned his binoculars to the truck's glove compartment and then retrieved the case of beer from the bed, thinking he ought to go inside to help speed along the proceedings. As he approached the barn, he heard faint cries of anguish. He dropped his beer and ran to the barn's side door. Slim tugged at the heavy door's modern steel handle and discovered that the door was locked. He pulled his cellphone from his pocket.

****

"Room, temperature up another 10 degrees," said Anne's voice through the studio's speakers. "For those of you keeping track, you're approaching 140 degrees now—I imagine you're feeling rather toasty. In a few minutes hyperthermia will set in, which as I understand it is considerably more lethal than its cooler cousin hypothermia. Of course, you may expire first from the aerosol version of the compound that I pumped into the studio with the gas dispersal device I installed yesterday in the barn's HVAC system. It could be that this colorless and odorless version of the compound I used on you all before is more toxic when inhaled slowly rather than ingested quickly. Either way, I think it prudent to thank you now for your participation as beta testers."

Weston struggled to form words as he writhed on the floor. "Just shut up already."

With tremendous effort, Kate raised her head to look at Anne's eyes on the screen. "If your quarrel is with me, then let my friends go."

The corner of Anne's eyes tightened, as if she were smirking. "That's very noble, but my quarrel is with all of you. I originally intended to insinuate myself into your coterie as a means of explicating how you were able to thwart the plans of my associates time and time again, though I soon realized it was just dumb luck on your part and intractable stupidity on theirs. However, you should take solace in the fact that I chose to accelerate my plan. I had thought to do this tomorrow during your wedding ceremony, but I have no wish for innocent people to die—just you five."

H.P. gasped for breath. "Why…are you…doing this?"

"Oh, simple, sensitive H.P. You once told me I had the eyes of Marlene Dietrich. Eyes are a funny thing—they're relatively small, but they see the whole world. Our culture has convinced itself that writers are still necessary, but only a few…and it's not too particular about their talents, or in your case and that of your writing partner, lack thereof. I mean really, could most readers today even tell the difference between a talented writer like me and hacks like you two?"

Becky twisted toward the screen. "Sure—you're crazy."

"Maybe, but as Aristotle wrote: There is no great genius without some touch of madness. At least I think that's what he wrote…it's all Greek to me."

"Jesus, your jokes are the worst torture of all," said Weston.

"And the level of your self-importance is staggering," added Kate.

"But," H.P. gasped, "I still don't…understand why."

"Because our society, to its great detriment, has become obsessed with screens over the last hundred years. Where once the written word elevated, the moving picture now degrades."

Edwin gulped at the air near the beverage refrigerator. "This is all just some fascist literacy crusade?"

Hearing the position of her fiancé's voice in the room, Kate opened her eyes, turned toward him, and whispered, "Eddie, can you reach my purse on top of the fridge?"

Anne focused on Edwin. "Yes, in a manner of speaking...think what the world might become with no more screened devices—another Enlightenment borne of a new dark age."

With his eyes shut, Edwin crawled toward the small refrigerator. He attempted to lift himself up but quickly collapsed to the floor from acute heat exhaustion. He reached above him and clutched the refrigerator's handle, openings its door. The blast of cool air invigorated him, and he slowly rose to his knees, snagging the purse by its strap. "I've got it."

Anne watched Edwin's effort with interest. "Mr. Hubert, I don't believe I have your full attention."

"There's a pair of yellow-lensed...glasses in there," said Kate. "Put them on."

"How very clever of you to come prepared," Anne complimented. "Those lenses should mitigate the effects of the gas, but light beyond the blue wavelength of the visible spectrum will still trigger the compound. There's no known cure beyond not drinking water or breathing air that's been contaminated...or learning to use a Braille screen, I suppose—and as for your current circumstances, your husband-to-be still has to contend with the heat."

Edwin found a case in the small purse and donned the glasses. "I can see...but I still can't breathe."

Kate weakly waved her arm. "Go...save yourself."

"I am truly touched by this display. You really do love the big lug." Anne's eyes moved back and forth on the screen as she shook her head. "Personally, I don't get what you see in him. Mr. Hubert, before you roll yourself all the way over to the door, you should know that it's locked with an internal deadbolt, which is currently under my exclusive control."

"Ed," said Weston, "there's an ax...in the back closet."

Edwin crawled as fast as he could manage toward the back of the studio. Uncapping a bottle of water from the bin of sports drinks near the utility closet, he quickly drank down half its contents and poured the rest over his head like a marathoner. He rose unsteadily to his feet, opened the door to the closet, and located the ax. Dragging the ax, he lumbered toward the side door.

Weston's cellphone vibrated in his pocket. He pulled out his phone and blindly tapped at the screen until he heard a voice. "Slim, is that you?"

"Yeah, it sounds like y'all could use some help. I'm outside trying to get in, but this old barn is built like a fortress. Can you open the side door?"

"It's a work in progress...but we're running out of time." Weston's parched mouth could barely make sound. "We need you to get in your pickup and smash into the front corner of the barn? I'm not kidding...just drive right through it so that we can get some fresh air in here."

"I would, but my truck is blocked in by your car and Kate's."

"Use my car then...the keys are in it."

As Weston heard Slim's footfalls through the phone, Edwin reached the side door and strained to raise the ax head above his waist. He dropped the blade on the door's handle, but it didn't budge. He breathed deeply, marshalling the last of his strength. He raised the ax above his head and chopped down on the handle, knocking it to the floor.

"I admit, I'm impressed," said Anne. "I didn't think you had it in you. You've won your freedom...for now, though I doubt there's time enough to drag the others to safety."

Weston heard the familiar revving of his car's engine outside. "Witch, we've got all the time we need."

Weston's sedan came crashing through the corner of the barn, destroying the screen on the front wall. The five inhaled deeply as the hot air and gas in the barn was exhausted out into the cold. Weston crawled to his crumpled car as the others slowly moved toward the barn's side door. Slim struggled to extricate himself from the wreckage as Weston feebly yanked on the handle of the driver's side door. Slim waved him off. "Get out of here...I can climb through the other side."

Weston nodded. He stumbled across the studio and out of the barn, falling to the ground with the others. For several moments, the only sound that could be heard was deep breathing and creaking wood. H.P. was the first to speak. "Weston...was that your car that Slim used to ram into the barn?"

"Yeah...his vehicle was blocked in."

"He should've used mine," said H.P. "I was thinking of getting a new car soon anyway...the keys were in the ignition."

Slim rounded the now-demolished corner of the barn. "The good news is that as you can plainly see, I was able to get out of your car. The bad news is that I had to kick the mangled passenger's side door off its hinges to do it. I'm fairly sure that old chariot of yours is bound for the scrapheap."

Chapter 51

As police officers took individual statements in the living room of the ranch house from the five who'd been trapped inside the barn, Slim spoke with the commanding officer. "Since she was linked in via a video feed, she could be anywhere. It'll take my digital forensics team time to follow the trail, by which point she could be anywhere else."

Slim shook his head. "Nah, she's close by. The others told me she mentioned installing the gas dispersal device yesterday, and I know from experience she's a DIY type who prefers to be near the action."

The C.O. nodded. "There's been plenty of action out here this past month…past year for that matter. Her father's death, though ruled exposure by the medical examiner, never set right with me. Now, given his daughter's activities of late, I'm thinking Ms. Hedonia might've had something to do with that too."

"I wouldn't be surprised. I get the sense that she's the type who wouldn't let little things like family bonds get in the way of achieving her objectives."

"Yeah, I get that same sense." The C.O. crossed her arms. "We have this house listed as her last known address, but I've got a tech searching databases for any previous residences…I'll let you know if we get a hit."

"I sure would appreciate it." Slim turned toward his friends. "It looks your officers are wrapping up their interviews, so I'm gonna go check on my people."

"Your people are awful lucky to have a friend like you."

"Thanks." Slim stepped down into the sunken portion of the living room as a few police officers stood and closed their notepads and laptops. "This is one helluva of a New Year's Eve party."

Becky sighed. "Figures—my first NYE in years without my kids, and it's a complete disaster before midnight."

"We've still got fondue," said Kate, "and all the wine we can drink."

"And a police chaperone," added Slim. "There'll be a technician working the crime scene out in the barn overnight as well as a patrol officer stationed in the driveway with personal orders from me to shoot out the kneecaps of anyone who attempts to leave. Everything will be gravy so long as you all stay here tonight."

"But what about tomorrow?" asked Edwin. "We've got guests coming…should we cancel the ceremony?"

Kate frowned. "I don't care if we have to get married under a bridge—we're not canceling our wedding."

"If you still had a mind to get hitched inside a barn," said Slim, "my trailer happens to be barn adjacent. It ain't high-tech like the one out there, but it's pretty in a rustic sort of way."

Kate smiled. "That sounds perfect."

"All right then, I'll give the farmer whose property it is a call, but he's let me park my trailer out there for over a year now, so I doubt he'd have a problem with us using his barn for a day."

Edwin stood and patted Slim on the shoulder. "Thank you, young man."

The commanding officer approached Slim. "We found a prior address for Ms. Hedonia. It looks like she hasn't lived there for some time, but the loft is still owned by her father's estate, so we're going to drive into the city to check it out. You're welcome to ride along."

"I'm ready."

Chapter 52

Anne typed away at her laptop on the kitchen counter in her loft when an email with the subject line—URGENT!—popped up from the moderator. She let out a sigh before agreeing to chat with him in his virtual meeting room. She'd had it up to her eyeballs with his virtual meetings, but she figured it shrewd to learn what he knew…or at least what he thought he did.

"I appreciate your willingness to meet with me on such short notice. I've got most of the council standing by in my virtual waiting room, and they're insistent on getting some answers."

"Answers about what?" asked Anne.

"About another botched attempt to eliminate the same small group that has stymied multiple operations of this council over the last couple of years. About preliminary reports of a compound being used in that attempt, which sounds remarkably similar to the one you'd told me was no longer extant. You know, the authorities will swab the air vents and undoubtedly analyze any residue they find. Once the formula is uploaded into the WHO database, there won't be any place in the world where that compound can be used again without being detected. And finally, there's a private matter that I'd like to discuss with you; I've yet to receive access to my fifteen percent stake in your offshore holding company despite having entered my personal information several days ago on the website for which you emailed me the link."

Anne raised her eyebrows, impressed with how quickly the moderator's police contacts had informed him of the incident in question, which had only occurred a couple of hours prior. "That compound was created at my expense, which makes it my concern—not the council's. As for the so-called botched attempt, it's not like this is the first time that's happened…at this point it's practically a tradition with the council, so let's call this strike two for me. And as far as your fifteen percent, you're not attempting to make an ATM transaction…there are layers of security protocols to be considered, so please be patient."

"I can be patient," said the moderator, "but I'm not so sure about the council. They're calling for blood— literally."

"Why do I have the feeling that you informed the council of what happened tonight, fomenting a demand for my ouster so that you could position yourself as my only protection against the angry mob?"

The moderator was silent for a moment. "Everyone has their own perspective."

"And their own price it would seem. How much is it going to cost me this time for you to intercede on my behalf?"

"I like the way you say 'half'…has a nice ring to it. My stake in your holding company has just increased from fifteen to fifty percent…or I feed you to the wolves—my offer is not negotiable."

"Fine."

"Good, I'm glad you see it my way," replied the moderator, "but you'll still have to address the council and explain yourself. I suggest you begin with groveling, then transition into pleading, and finally strike a note of contriteness mixed with a soupçon of optimism for our future. I'll speak up when the shouts of 'off with her head' become deafening."

"How very considerate of you."

Anne listened as several chimes announced the entrance to the virtual meeting room of the waiting council members.

"Welcome," said the moderator in a haughty tone. "As I've informed you previously, we have a matter of some urgency to discuss tonight, so—"

"Hey, Francis, shut up for a minute," interrupted Anne, "or do you prefer to go by Frank? You didn't specify when you divulged your personal information to gain access to that dummy holding company of mine. You see, he wanted a fifteen percent stake to keep you morons in line, but just now he upped his ask to fifty. What do I care? Half of nothing is still nothing." In a small window open on her computer screen, Anne noticed a police officer coming into view of the security camera located near the downstairs entrance. "Anyway, I have someplace to be, so I'm going to go, but I thought you idiots might like to know your moderator's name before I left. I'm entering his surname into the chat box now along with some other personal information he unwittingly gave me. As for the rest of you halfwits, I don't know your names, but I know what you've been up to; I've got all your dirty little schemes outlined in the dossier I'm holding, which I intend to turn over to the police along with Frank's contact info. You can come looking for me if you like, but I think after the authorities read this dossier and talk with Frank, they'll connect the dots to you all without too much trouble. Our esteemed moderator doesn't strike me as the strong, silent type, so I imagine you'll be getting a knock on your door sooner than you'll be able to find mine—besides, isn't Francis really the one to blame for this mess? I mean, he is the one who vouched for me in the first place. Either way, no hard feelings—bye now."

Anne closed her laptop and tucked it under her arm, leaving the dossier on the counter. She crossed the loft's open space to the far window, grabbed her backpack from the sill, and exited down the fire escape.

Chapter 53

Since no one felt particularly conversational after their ordeal, the five elected to have their fondue in the living room with the radio on. As the others speared bits of bread and fruit with long forks, H.P. tuned in stations with the remote. "What are you guys in the mood for— classical…classic rock?"

"Something without lyrics, please," said Edwin. "I have a hard time hearing people talk over people singing."

H.P. scanned radio stations on the stereo as he looked longingly at the large television hanging on the wall above it. "Even though the effects of the gas weren't as intense, the thought of turning on the TV still makes me nauseous, but it's too bad we can't watch a movie. I imagine it would look and sound great in here."

"I'm wiped," said Becky. "I'm not sure I could stay awake long enough to finish a movie anyway."

Weston poked at a cube of sourdough on the coffee table. "Besides, it'll be midnight in little over an hour, and I want to hear the program for the fireworks at Navy Pier."

"Okay then," H.P. replied, "I'll see if any of the AM stations are covering the fireworks, though I can't imagine what the play by play will be like…there goes another one—very twinkly."

Edwin lifted a strawberry from the chocolate fondue

pot. "If you can't find radio coverage, we could watch a broadcast of the fireworks on a local channel and turn off the picture."

Kate dabbed the corner of her mouth with her napkin. "My company is having a charity event at Navy Pier tonight. We could've had waterfront seats to see the fireworks."

Weston leaned back in a recliner. "These seats are just fine for me tonight."

"What's the event for?" asked Becky.

"They're hosting a gala in the ballroom of the Terminal Building to raise money for several local libraries," answered Kate. "As one of the vice presidents who interviewed me put it, there'll be 'several visiting politicians and dysenteries' in attendance."

Becky contemplatively stirred the cheese fondue with her fork. "Is the goal to raise money for new books?"

Kate slowly shook her head. "No...sort of the opposite really. Their aim is to modernize the libraries, updating them with computers and high-speed Internet access."

H.P. pressed the mute button on the remote. "You know, I didn't give it much thought at the time—being too busy thinking I was about to die—but now that I replay it in my head, the way Anne called us beta testers sounded...odd."

"How do you mean?" asked Edwin. "She was testing out that compound on us, like we were her beta testers."

H.P. nodded. "Sure, but that's the second time we've been exposed to it...she already knew it would work."

"Maybe she wasn't so sure since this time she got us with gas," said Weston.

"Maybe," H.P. replied, "but it could also be that what she actually wanted to test was the gas dispersal device she installed in the barn's HVAC system."

Becky touched her chin with her index finger. "Which might be the real reason she wanted to gas us today instead of tomorrow."

"But she told us she accelerated her plan so as not to harm innocent people at our wedding," said Edwin.

"Right...because Anne's such a humanitarian." Weston rolled his eyes. "By the way, Ed, I was being sarcastic."

"I was eighty percent sure," Edwin replied. "She did express negative opinions about the ubiquity of screens and how they've displaced book reading...an event to promote the supplanting of library books with electronic devices would seem an apposite venue to air her grievances."

"As well as afford her an opportunity to undermine her father's company and the executives who work there," added Kate, "for whom, given her decisions during the brief tenure of her presidency, she demonstrably did not harbor the best of intentions."

Chapter 54

The five diffidently entered the side door of the barn, the front corner of which was covered by a large sheet of plastic.

"Knock, knock," said Kate.

A crime scene technician wearing a hazmat suit atop a ladder looked down.

Becky waved up at the tech. "I hope we're not catching you at an inopportune moment."

The tech descended the ladder and removed his safety hood. "I'd planned to spend tonight with my girlfriend—we had reservations at a pricey nightclub…instead I'm spending New Year's Eve taking residue samples from the ventilation system of a structurally compromised barn, so I wouldn't exactly call any of this an opportune moment."

Weston nodded. "Gosh, that sounds almost as bad as nearly being murdered."

H.P. held up his hands. "Before we all get off on the wrong foot, what we came out here to ask you—and then I promise we'll be out of your hair—is if there's anything you can tell us about the gas dispersal device that you found installed in the vents."

The tech shrugged. "It's a device for dispersing gas. What else do you want to know?"

"You must've seen these types of gadgets before," said Becky. "Do you get the sense that this one was installed by a pro?"

The tech shook his head. "Not really…it was a pretty jerry-rigged installation."

"Like maybe the installer hadn't done it before," Kate said, "so this might be sort of a test run to make sure it'd work."

The tech sighed. "I don't know about all that…I mean maybe. This stuff isn't rock science, but it's not necessarily intuitive either—the perp probably pulled instructions off the Internet, but you know how reliable those can be."

"Quite unreliable has been my experience," said Edwin.

H.P. rubbed the back of his neck. "So it likely wasn't installed by a preeminent petrologist or someone with extensive HVAC training."

"That's a fair assumption," replied the tech, "though to say anything beyond that would be pure speculation."

"I suppose that's better than the diluted kind," Weston replied.

"Is it though?" asked Edwin.

Kate waved goodbye to the tech as she ushered the others toward the door. "As promised, we'll let you get back to your job, but feel free to come inside the house to take a coffee break whenever you like."

The five huddled on the path between the barn and the main house, some stomping the gravel to keep their feet warm.

"I wouldn't characterize that as a revelatory exchange," said Edwin.

"All the pieces seem to indicate that Anne intends to ring in the New Year with a bang," Weston replied, "but then again, we might be getting ready to embark on a wild ghost chase."

H.P. shook his head. "I believe the phrase is 'wild goose chase.' "

Weston frowned. "I'm pretty sure I could catch a goose."

"If there's a chance that we might prevent Anne from doing something terrible, then we have to try," said Kate.

Edwin nodded. "I quite agree, my dear."

"But could we even make it all the way to the lake from out here by midnight?" asked Becky. "The traffic in and around the city must be horrible right now."

Weston eyed the officer sitting in his squad car parked in front of the house. "We do have a police escort."

"I believe he was tasked with watching us," said Edwin, "not chauffeuring us around."

Weston smiled. "He can't very well watch us if we drive away and he stays behind."

H.P. tugged on his earlobe. "What you're proposing is a pursuit—not an escort."

"Regardless," said Weston, "the other drivers on the road will see the police lights and dutifully make way for us."

"Let's take my car—it's got more airbags." Kate handed Weston her keys. "You drive."

Chapter 55

As Weston weaved through the braking cars on the interstate, he adjusted the rearview mirror to reduce the reflection from the strobing red and blue lights. His cellphone rang. Edwin picked it up from the cupholder in the center console. "It's Slim."

"Put him on speaker," said Weston.

"Weston, have you been providing that officer parked in front of the house booze? I ask because I just got a call from him reporting that he's currently chasing after you down the expressway at a high rate of speed, and the only reason I can figure he'd give such a ridiculous report is because he's drunk."

Weston shook his head. "Slim, I can't talk right now. I'm driving down the expressway at a high rate of speed."

"Slim, it's Becky. We think Anne might be planning an attack at Navy Pier."

"So why the hell didn't you call me?"

"We figured you were still busy trying to track Anne to her last known address," said Kate.

H.P. leaned forward from the backseat between Kate and Becky. "Besides, it's a pretty half-baked theory."

"Were you able apprehend her?" asked Edwin.

"No," Slim answered, "but we know she was here. She left behind some documents that contain, if it all checks out, a lot of incriminating evidence."

"Why would she do that?" asked Kate.

"I imagine because she has an ax to grind," Slim replied. "I get the sense that Ms. Hedonia wasn't fond of her co-conspirators."

Becky shook her head. "I get the sense that she's not fond of anyone—a real misanthrope."

"You might be right about that," said Slim.

"Oh, Weston," Edwin blurted, "that'd make a great name for a villainess in your next book—Miss Anthrope."

"Anyway, the local police are still working the scene here," Slim said, "but I'll make my way over to Navy Pier to meet you."

"You think what we're doing actually makes sense?" asked Weston.

"I think it makes about as much sense as a striped dalmatian, but I've learned to play along with your hunches over the past couple of years."

"10-4," Weston replied.

"I'll call the officer chasing after you all and apprise him of the situation, so—as a courtesy—let him get in front of you."

"Much appreciated, young man," said Edwin.

"Sure thing, just do me a favor—stay safe and keep in contact."

"Slim, that's two favors," said Weston.

"A third favor specifically for you comes to mind that involves sticking your smart remarks where the sun don't shine, but it wouldn't be polite to mention in mixed company."

Chapter 56

Not wanting to run the risk of being recognized by one of the employees of her father's company, Anne chose not to enter Navy Pier's Terminal Building where the gala ball was being held, opting instead to access the HVAC system via the roof. After cutting the padlock on the metal gate covering the bottom of the safety cage, she climbed the fixed ladder up the three stories. Even on such a chilly night, her weighty backpack caused her to break a sweat by the time she reached the roof. The dispersal device and aerosol canister were considerably heavier than the crystalline version of the compound had been when she'd climbed the water tower.

Having studied the schematics of the Terminal Building, Anne quickly found a suitable HVAC access point and set to work installing the device. As she had hoped, having performed the installation previously made her feel more confident about the assembly process, though the building's vast ventilation system required an industrial-level dispersal device, and while the two devices worked on the same principles, the second required many more mounting components, which in turn would require more time.

****

Slim and the police officer who drove him to Navy Pier approached the security kiosk. The uniformed man looked up from behind his desk. "Can I help you two?"

Slim nodded. "We got a tip that somebody might be trying to monkey with the ventilation system in the Terminal Building."

"Can you call a member of your maintenance team and have them meet us in the lobby?" asked the officer.

"No problem." The security guard picked up the phone on his desk. "We'll do whatever we can to assist— just don't ask us to clear the pier right before the fireworks."

****

Weston parked behind their police escort at Navy Pier's front entrance. He took his cellphone from the cupholder and called Slim. "Hey, we're here. Where are you?"

"Me, another cop, and a maintenance guy are checking the HVAC access points around the perimeter of the grand ballroom, but so far we ain't found nothing."

"Do you want us to come help?" asked Weston.

"No, there's already three of us poking our heads into vents and shining flashlights around…it ain't a job that requires a big group."

"Maybe you haven't found anything because Anne's not here yet."

"That, or maybe she ain't coming at all."

"Yeah, I suppose that's a possibility too." Weston turned to look at Edwin and then the others in the backseat. "We'll split up and search the pier. Call if you find anything."

"You do the same."

Weston slid his phone into his pocket. "Ed, why don't you and the ladies look for Anne along the boardwalk? H.P. and I will look for her around the outside of the Terminal Building."

****

Slim returned his cellphone to his pocket. He watched as the maintenance man unlocked another access panel with a key from a retractable, janitor's sized keyring. He took note of all the people walking in the hallway dressed in tuxedos and gowns. He turned to the other police officer. "This is too out in the open, ain't it?"

The officer nodded. "Yeah, there's no way somebody could install the device you described into one of these ducts without getting noticed."

The maintenance worker opened the panel. "One of you two want to do the honors, or are we done for the night?"

"I'll have a looksee," said Slim. "This might all just be a snipe hunt, but then again you never know."

"Nope, you never do," agreed the other officer.

****

Becky, Kate, and Edwin spread out in a line to comb through the multitudes thronging the boardwalk, waiting for the fireworks to begin. Becky caught Kate's attention in the distance and shook her head. Edwin beckoned to both of them from the side of the boardwalk farthest from the water. Kate and Becky made their way out of the crowd to Edwin's less densely populated position.

"At this rate, we'll never find Anne before midnight," said Edwin, "if indeed that's when she plans to strike, which seems most likely."

Becky nodded. "In all these people, I'm not sure we'd find her before sunrise, so what do you suggest?"

Edwin pointed up. "Higher ground."

Kate looked at the colossal Ferris wheel over Edwin's shoulder. "The Centennial Wheel could give us the vantage point we need to spot her."

****

Weston and H.P. walked past the Terminal Building toward the end of the pier. They turned to take in the full view of the building's façade, flanked by two towers at its rear that rose twice as high as the roofline.

"I don't see her," said Weston sardonically.

H.P. shook his head. "We probably couldn't find her in all these people if we had a whole day to look."

"I don't think she's down here among the hoi polloi. I believe our search strategy would benefit from some three-dimensional thinking."

H.P. tilted his head up toward the building's arched roof. "You're going to make me regret being on your search team, aren't you?"

****

As their gondola reached the apex of the Ferris wheel, Becky and Kate scanned the crowds below while Edwin marveled at the city's skyline in the distance.

"Eddie, do you really think Anne is standing on top of the Hancock Building?" asked Kate.

Edwin turned to reply to his fiancée, but before he did so, a shadowy figure wielding shiny tools on the roof of the Terminal Building caught his attention. "No, I think she's right over there."

Kate and Becky twisted in their seats to see where Edwin was pointing. Kate nearly jumped up with excitement. "Holy crap, that's her."

Becky took out her cellphone. "I'll call Slim."

****

The maintenance worker opened another access panel. Slim poked his head inside and shined his flashlight around—nothing. He stood up straight and switched off the flashlight. "Empty as the rest."

The maintenance man shook his head. "That's the last access point down here."

"What do you mean 'down here?' " asked Slim.

The maintenance worker looked up at the ceiling. "There's a few access points on the roof."

Slim turned to the other officer who nodded back. "That's where we should've started."

"Nah," said the maintenance man, "the only way up there is via a ladder that's covered by a gate with a big old padlock on it—besides, it's cold out there."

"I'm pretty sure our bad gal has bolt cutters and a warm coat." Slim answered his buzzing cellphone. "Go ahead, Becky...you don't say...by the south tower...we're on our way."

"Your friends spotted her?" asked the officer.

"Yep, on the other side of the building." Slim started to run down the hallway when his phone buzzed again. "Go ahead, Weston...you don't say...somebody cut the lock on a gate covering an access ladder...yeah, Becky just called—they spotted Anne on the roof by the south tower...wait for us, we're on our way."

****

Weston returned his cellphone to his pocket as H.P. stared up the ladder. "So what'd Slim say?"

"Apparently Anne's on the roof over by the south tower." Weston began climbing the ladder.

"Shouldn't we wait for Slim and the others?"

"No, he told us to go up without them...they've got our backs when they get here."

"I'm more concerned about our fronts since that'll be the part facing her."

"It's just one woman who's not even expecting us," said Weston. "What's to worry about?"

"You putting it that way makes me twice as worried."

****

Anne clamped the final mount into place. She slowly removed the aerosol canister from her backpack, careful not to knock the nozzle against anything that might cause the compound to prematurely discharge. She held the canister close to her chest as she leaned down and then bent over at the waist, lowering her upper torso into the ventilation shaft. She stretched out her arms, holding the canister with both hands. She could just reach the socket that the nozzle screwed into.

As Anne struggled to nest the canister into place, a thundering bang reverberated through the shaft, causing her to fumble the canister. *What was that,* she thought, *the fireworks shouldn't start for another few minutes.* She grabbed the canister before it rolled beyond her reach down the shaft. Anne lifted herself out of the vent to inspect the canister for damage and spotted Weston helping H.P. off the ductwork where he'd fallen some thirty yards away. "I might've known it was you two clumsy oafs making all that racket—not very sneaky."

"We don't need to sneak up on you," said Weston. "We've got you surrounded."

Anne looked around and grinned. "I don't see anyone else."

H.P. brushed himself off. "Well…they're on the way."

"And they'll be coming up the same ladder you did," added Weston. "There's no way down for you."

"Boys, down is always easier than up." Anne nodded to the backpack at her feet. "Especially when you've brought along a rope ladder. I can be on the ground and lost in that crowd facing the lake within seconds of the fireworks starting."

"How do you propose to anchor a ladder with us chasing after you?" asked Weston.

"I don't see that happening since I also brought along this." Anne pulled a small revolver from her pocket.

H.P. began to slowly raise his hands. "You don't really want to shoot us."

Anne leveled her gun at the pair. "Sorry, but I kinda do."

"Why are you raising your hands?" Weston asked. "She's not arresting us."

"I suppose I could sort of understand wanting to shoot Weston," said H.P.

"I'm loath to dispatch you two so prosaically, but I do have a schedule to keep." Anne abruptly became distracted by a low hissing noise "Oh hell." The nozzle atop the canister she held in her other hand exploded, quickly engulfing her in a cloud of dense smoke.

"Now's our chance to grab her," Weston whispered.

"Grab her?" asked H.P. "I can't even see her."

"And she can't see us to aim." Two shots rang out from the smoke. "She's firing blind. Let's circle around her on either side and try to get behind—" A third shot caused Weston to collapse in pain. "She got me...in the shin. Duck down...before she gets...you too."

H.P. pointed to the tower beyond the smoke. "Look—she's climbing up."

As Weston held his right knee to his chest, he turned toward the south tower to see Anne climbing the decorative lattice-like elements inlaid amid the brickwork. "What's she doing?"

"She's trying to get above the smoke," answered H.P. "She must be half blind."

"And double crazy—only in part because of the gas."

"I'm going after her."

"Why?" asked Weston. "There's nowhere she can go from the top of that tower. Her rope ladder can't be that long…and from here it doesn't even look like she's got her backpack on."

"She might get hurt."

"Might get hurt," Weston muttered in disbelief. "I'm hurt. I know you got hit by Cupid's arrow, but trust me—it doesn't feel nearly as painful as getting shot with an actual bullet."

Suddenly the two heard a deep concussive blast that they felt in their chests; they each craned their necks skyward to see the first salvo of fireworks burst into many vivid colors over the water, including brilliant blues of Bengal light. Amidst the cheers from below, they heard Anne scream from above—that same shrill scream they'd heard weeks before at her father's house. Losing her grip, Anne fell from the tower—down past the roofline to the base of the building. H.P. walked to the edge of the roof and peered over the side. "Her troubles, whatever they may have been, are now over."

"Then so are ours," Weston replied. "I'm glad this building proved terminal for her and not us. At least this time there won't be any doubt about her death…but, you know, I'm sorry for any loss you may be feeling—more's the pity, and all that."

H.P. ignored his friend's callous comments as he continued to stare downward. A small crowd began to gather around Anne's body. A man taking a video of the scene with his cellphone noticed H.P. on the roof above and called up to him. "Who was she?"

"Our state's poet laureate," answered H.P.

The man turned to the woman standing beside him. "Did you know Illinois had a poet laureate?"

The bemused woman shrugged.

Epilogue

The Pirate Hunter had swum to the GPS coordinates for the rendezvous to find the small submersible sent to extract him under attack from above by a pirate ship dropping depth charges. He watched helplessly as explosions in the distance lit up the dark water and tossed about the two-man sub. When the barrage of depth charges finally stopped, P.H. swam as close as he dared to the sinking vessel. Bubbles issuing from a crack in the hull indicated that the sub was foundering rather than maneuvering. As the craft took on more water, it would sink faster and faster, and if he wasn't careful pull him down too in the suction caused by cavitation.

P.H. paralleled the descent of the tiny sub as best he could, but soon it sank faster than he could dive and was swallowed by the darkness below. P.H. continued to dive down, hoping the sub had come to rest on an as yet unseen shelf rather than falling deeper into a trench. He thought there might still be a chance to rescue the submariners, if indeed they were still alive. However, as the deep waters grew colder and darker, P.H. knew he could descend no farther.

Something shining in the near distance caught his attention. The Pirate Hunter swam toward what he soon discovered was a whale boneyard resting atop a diminutive oceanic plateau. He hoped the little sub had somehow made its way over to the flat surface, but as he swam among the gargantuan skeletons, he found no evidence of anything manmade. *But what was it that had shined in the darkness?* P.H. wondered. He dove down closer to the bones, swimming through a ribcage larger than the submersible he'd been pursuing. The bones were eerily white—surgically cleaned by water and time.

Nestled in a coiled pile of immense vertebrae, he spotted a giant clam. The enormous bivalve slowly opened its shell to reveal a shiny pearl the size of a heavyweight's fist. The Pirate Hunter swam closer, but the shell closed again. P.H. waited near the massive mollusk, aware that his oxygen supply was running dangerously low. Finally the shell opened once more, its nacreous lining iridescent in the darkness. In the center of the clam rested the pearl, so lustrous that P.H. could see his hand reflected on its surface.

The Tridacna clamped downed on the Pirate Hunter's arm, holding him in a vise-like grip. He struggled to free himself, but he couldn't budge the shell even an inch. Soon his oxygen would be depleted. P.H. calmed his mind and relaxed his muscles. He removed one of his scuba fins, stretched his free arm over the top of the clam, and with the rigid fin firmly in hand, raked its scalloped points across the abductor muscle at the back of the shell that comprised the bivalve's hinge.

The giant clam released the Pirate Hunter, its shell now open wide. P.H. stared at the glimmering pearl for a moment but thought better of attempting another grab. He slipped the fin back on his foot and began swimming toward the surface, looking back only once to see the glowing pearl diminish in the frigid darkness.

****

H.P. awoke to the glow of his cellphone's screen.

He picked up his phone off the nightstand. The dean was calling. "Hello."

"You sound groggy."

"It was a late night."

"It must've been," said the dean. "It's nearly ten o'clock. Listen, I know it's a holiday, but I thought you'd appreciate beginning the New Year with some good news. Given recent developments that the chancellor was just made aware of, she's decided to reinstate you. You can start teaching again when the spring semester begins next week."

"No."

"No?"

H.P. stared at the bits of peeling paint hanging from his bedroom ceiling. "I'll be glad to teach again in the fall, but for next semester I was really looking forward to that sabbatical you mentioned...to start writing some new ideas I've had lately."

A long pause followed before the dean spoke again. "I'm afraid there's no provision in your contract for a sabbatical...I was only trying to put a positive spin on you being placed on administrative leave—highlighting the silver lining, so to speak."

"I see."

"So we can expect you back on campus next week?"

"No, just keep me on administrative leave then," H.P. answered, "or fire me. Either way, I'll be available in the fall if you want me back."

"I'm afraid you have me at a loss for words...I don't know what to say."

"I do—may you and Charity have a happy New Year."

****

Weston entered the barn on crutches, the right leg of his tuxedo trousers cut to the knee to accommodate his cast. He spotted H.P. sitting atop a straw bale and hobbled in his direction. "Don't you look smart...by that I mean well dressed, not intelligent."

H.P. looked up. "I think we already did that joke."

"You said it about me; now I'm saying it about you."

"Then I suppose it makes sense that I would've said it first."

Weston gingerly took a seat on the bale. "Speaking of great minds thinking alike."

"I think it's more an instance of fools seldom differing."

"Whatever...if you're still free for the next few months, we should get started on the follow-up to our award-winning book...though perhaps this time we refrain from a protracted, multipart epilogue. A story's ending should be a period...not an ellipsis."

H.P. nodded. "Maybe down the road. For now, I'm going to do some writing on my own. I've had a few thoughts recently for my Pirate Hunter that I'd like to explore."

"I thought you put that character to bed."

"I did, but he seems to have woken up."

"I'm glad for it, my friend." Weston glanced up as Edwin and Slim approached. "You two did a terrific job cleaning this barn...it's like a hundred times nicer in here than your trailer parked outside."

"Thanks...I guess," said Slim. "Setting up the propane heaters took the most time."

Edwin looked around approvingly. "We didn't get to sleep in today like you two, but I think the results are worth it."

"I would've been here to help, but I just got done getting patched up at the hospital." Weston tapped the cast on his leg with a crutch and then turned to H.P. "What's your excuse?"

H.P. sighed. "Since you were in the hospital, and I was the only other eyewitness to Anne's demise, the police had a number of questions for me. I didn't make it home until just before dawn."

Weston leaned his crutches against the bale. "That's all right...you probably wouldn't have been much help anyway."

"I got a call from a buddy of mine with Chicago P.D. a little while ago," said Slim. "They found a few Molotov cocktails in Ms. Hedonia's backpack. They figure that when she got back down to ground level from the rooftop, she was planning to toss them into the ballroom—cook everybody alive while they were writhing around, like she tried to do you all...except this time, flame-broiled instead of roasted."

Weston shook his head. "What a witch."

"I trust you're not talking about me." Becky approached with an attractive, middle-aged woman wearing an identical dress. "We just came from helping Kate get ready in Slim's trailer. She'll be out soon; her other bridesmaid is applying the final touches. Anyway, I'd like to introduce you all to Lauren Ipsum, Kate's college roommate."

"Oh, the theater major," said H.P.

Lauren smiled. "I ended up double majoring in theater and English. I teach creative writing at a community college. In fact, I'd love to pick your brain sometime about your Pirate Hunter character...maybe over a drink."

"I think we have time for a glass of punch before the ceremony begins." H.P. stood from the bale. "Besides, my straw allergies are starting to get the better of me."

Becky sat down next to her husband as H.P. and Lauren headed in the direction of the punchbowl. "Weddings are a good place to meet people; everyone looks presentable and is on their best behavior…well, almost everyone." Lance and Van approached—their suits covered in straw. "What happened to you two?"

"We were jumping from the hayloft onto a huge pile of straw in the back," answered Lance.

Van brushed straw from his necktie. "But we thought we'd check in to see if there's an ETA on the bride yet."

"She'll be out in a few minutes," said Becky. "Don't make me regret not leaving you two at home with your aunt and sister…calm down and catch your breath before the ceremony begins."

"No more horseplay until the reception," added Weston.

"Shouldn't the phrase be 'pony play' instead?" asked Lance. "You know, since it's alliterative."

Slim put a hand on his hip. "I'll be…you send one boy to college, and somehow they both turn into brainiacs."

"Vance, with the spring semester beginning soon," said Edwin, "I'm curious if you're still planning to change your major."

"It's funny, when I was cramming for my finals, I really started getting into all that Ag stuff, so I think I'll stick with it for a while."

"That sounds like a mighty fine idea," said Slim.

Weston grinned. "Maybe someday you'll be parking

your trailer next to his barn."

"If it's my barn," said Van, "you'd be welcome to park inside."

"Much appreciated."

Edwin licked his lips. "I'm parched…why don't we have some punch too before the ceremony begins?"

"You all go ahead," replied Becky. "Me and Mr. Pegleg are going to sit right here for a spell."

Weston wrapped his arm around his wife. "I don't know who my Becca is calling a pegleg. I plan on requesting a Heavy D song to dance to during the reception." Van rolled his eyes as he, Lance, Slim, and Edwin turned toward the punchbowl. "You know, this isn't a bad way to kick off the new year."

Becky rested her head on Weston's shoulder. "A truly happy beginning."

A word about the author...

Wesley Payton has a B.A. in Rhetoric/Philosophy and an M.A. in English. He has been a short-story presenter for the Illinois Philological Association. His play *Way Station* was selected for a Next Draft reading in 2015, and *What Does a Question Weigh?* was selected for a staged reading as part of the 2017 Chicago New Work Festival. He is the author of the novels *Lead Tears, Darkling Spinster, Darkling Spinster No More, Standing in Doorways, Raison Deidre, Oblong, Intimate Recreation, Downstate Illinois, The House Painter and the Pirate Hunter, Immurdered: Some Time to Kill,* and *Dissimiles: More's the Pity.*

Wesley and his family live in Oak Park, Illinois. Find out more about Wesley and his books here: http://wespayton.weebly.com/

Thank you for purchasing
this publication of The Wild Rose Press, Inc.

For questions or more information
contact us at
info@thewildrosepress.com.

The Wild Rose Press, Inc.
www.thewildrosepress.com